D O W N S I D E R S

DOWNSIDERS

A NOVEL BY

NEAL SHUSTERMAN

SIMON & SCHUSTER BOOKS FOR YOUNG READERS

For Joelle

Acknowledgments

I'd like to thank the following Topsiders for helping to bring this book to the surface... The Fictionaires, and particularly Don Stanwood for his wealth of subterranean information; Keith Richardson, Lauri Dudley, and Joseph Brennan for their research assistance; my sons, Brendan and Jarrod, for being the story's first audience; my wife, Elaine, for her endless support and wealth of ideas; and Stephanie Owens Lurie, whose editorial brilliance earns her the title of First Wise Advisor.

SIMON & SCHUSTER BOOKS FOR YOUNG READERS

An imprint of Simon & Schuster Children's Publishing Division

1230 Avenue of the Americas, New York, New York 10020

Design by Heather Wood

The text of this book is set in Minion. Printed in the United States of America

10 9 8 7 6 5 4 3 2 1

Library of Congress Cataloging-in-Publication Data

Shusterman, Neal.

Downsiders / by Neal Shusterman.—1st ed.

p. cm.

Summary: When fourteen-year-old Lindsay meets Talon and discovers
the Downsiders world which had evolved from the subway built in New York in 1867
by Alfred Ely Beach, she and her new friend experience the clash of their two cultures.

ISBN 0-689-80375-3 (hc.)

[1. Subways—New York (State)—New York—Fiction. 2. New York (N.Y.)—Fiction.] I. Title.

PZ7.S55987Do 1999   [Fic]—dc21   98-38555

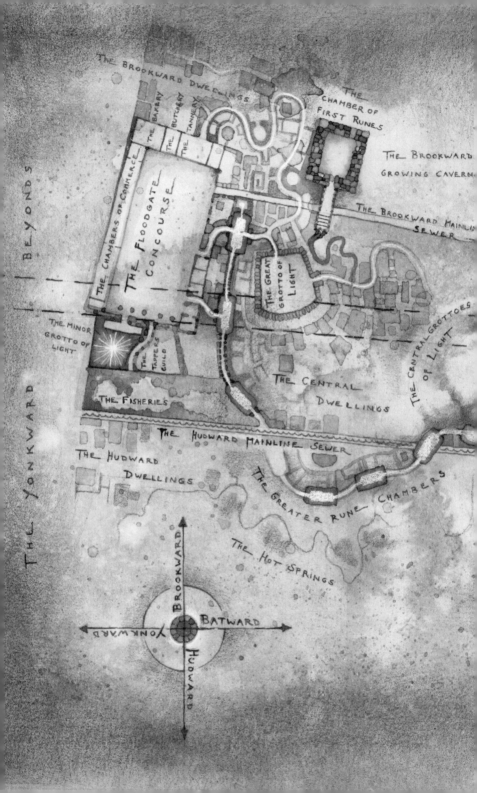

THE BROOKWARD DWELLINGS

THE CHAMBER OF FIRST RUNES

THE BAKERY
THE BUTCHERY
THE TANNERY

THE BROOKWARD GROWING CAVERN

THE CHAMBERS OF COMMERCE

THE FLOODGATE CONCOURSE

THE BROOKWARD MAINLINE SEWER

THE GREAT GROTTO OF LIGHT

THE MINOR GROTTO OF LIGHT

THE TAPPERS GUILD

THE CENTRAL GROTTOES OF LIGHT

THE CENTRAL DWELLINGS

THE FISHERIES

THE HUDWARD MAINLINE SEWER

THE HUDWARD DWELLINGS

THE GREATER RUNE CHAMBERS

THE HOT SPRINGS

BEYOND S

THE YONKWARD

BROOKWARD

BATWARD

YONKWARD

HUDWARD

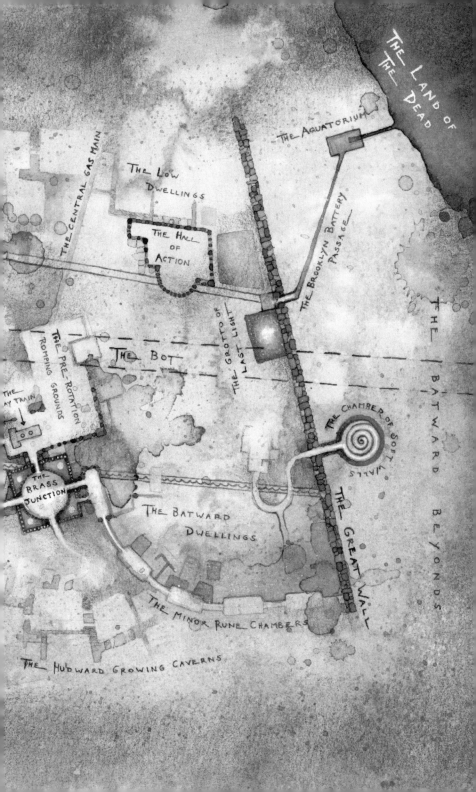

THE LAND OF THE DEAD

THE AQUATORIUM

THE CENTRAL GAS MAIN

THE LOW DWELLINGS

THE HALL of ACTION

THE BROOKLYN BATTERY PASSAGE

THE PRE-ROTATION ROMPING GROUNDS

THE BOT

THE GROTTO of LAST LIGHT

THE BATWARD BEYONDS

THE MY TRAIN

THE CHAMBER of SOFT WALLS

THE BRASS JUNCTION

THE BATWARD DWELLINGS

THE GREAT WALL

THE MINOR RUNE CHAMBERS

THE HUDWARD GROWING CAVERNS

Once Below a Time

Cities are never random.

No matter how chaotic they might seem, everything about them grows out of a need to solve some problem. In fact, a city is nothing more than a solution to a problem, that in turn creates more problems that need more solutions, until towers rise, roads widen, bridges are built, and millions of people are caught up in a mad race to feed the problem-solving, problem-creating frenzy.

Even the structure of a city is no accident. To look at New York, one might think the whole skyline was haphazard: an outcrop of skyscrapers downtown, followed by smaller buildings, giving way to skyscrapers again at Midtown—like two mountains with a valley in between. But if you studied the earth beneath the city, you'd know the reason for this structure: The city is built atop an underground mountain range, and only where the granite peaks come close to the surface, is the earth sturdy enough to hold skyscrapers. The shape of the skyline is no accident at all—it's a perfect mirror of the unseen mountains below.

Hiding below the surface are many more solutions to the woes of civilization—from hundreds of miles of subway lines, to thousands of miles of utility tunnels, all so twisted and confused that no Topsider can truly know what lies beneath.

Or *who* lies beneath.

As in the sea, where strange and mysterious creatures thrive on thermal vents in the deepest trenches, a deep city Downside grew; a place where people learned to thrive separately and apart from a world ruled by the sun. In time those people grew strong and noble, for nobility was the only way to save themselves from the despair of a life without sky. Of course, that isn't to say they were any wiser than Topsiders. Just like anyone else, their potential for profound stupidity ran deep. But unlike most surface dwellers, the Downsiders nurtured in their hearts a bright and untainted innocence. That innocence alone made them like few others on this shrinking planet—and who's to say whether things would still be the same had it not been for the Great Shaft Disaster, and the power of a single chance meeting to change the world.

The year is now, the month is December. And it all began last night....

NEAL SHUSTERMAN

1

Talon

High above the windblown city, a drop of falling rain was caught by an icy blast and puffed into a feathery flake of snow. No longer did it plunge through the city, but instead drifted slowly toward the magnificent lights of a New York night.

It sailed past the tip of the Empire State Building, whose upper floors were lit a Christmas green and red. Then, caught in a crosswind, the flake sailed further uptown, spinning around the icicle spire of the Chrysler Building and drifting down toward the late-night traffic of Forty-second Street. At 11:00, from high above, one might think the streets of the city truly were paved with gold, for the roofs of the taxis were like great golden bricks as they sat waiting for the light on Lexington Avenue.

Sheltered from the high winds, the flake wafted undisturbed down the face of Grand Central Station and landed on the tip of the nose of a young man who sat firmly on the bottom rung of life's ladder.

His name and destiny are of little importance, but he does command some attention here, for the sole reason that his life is about to end.

All of nineteen years old, but with a hopeless weariness that made him seem many years older, he huddled in a stone niche, near the great train station's entrance. He did not bother to shake out the snow that now speckled his hair.

People ignored him as he sat in the lonely corner. The well-dressed men and women in the city were skilled in looking the other way when they came across a derelict bit of humanity. To the business folk in camel-hair coats and Armani shoes, the bums of the city were unfortunate by-products of their lives—like the mountains of trash that accumulated each time the sanitation workers went on strike—so they simply turned their noses up and kept on walking.

Tonight the young man did not extend his cup for spare change. He wanted no one's money anymore, no one's pity. His will to live was quickly failing him, and by morning his will, and his life, would extinguish in the cold, like a street-light flickering out at dawn.

As he sat there, searching for a reason to be, he caught a pair of eyes watching him from a storm drain across the street. In truth, those eyes had been watching him patiently for more than an hour, studying his actions—or lack of action. Only now, in the headlight glare of a bus changing lanes, did he see those eyes regarding him from beneath the curb across Forty-second Street. The face appeared young—

younger than he—but in an instant the bus crossed in front of him and, when it passed, the storm drain was just a dark slit in the curb once more.

With the numbness of his fingers and toes slowly growing into his wrists and ankles, he dug up the will to rise to his feet. Then he shuffled into the warmth of Grand Central Station, still trying to figure out if the face he saw in the drain was truly there or just an image dredged up from his own troubled mind.

There were others like him occupying the warmer corners of the station. Most were older, indigents without a penny to their name who stood little chance of finding their way back into a productive life. Some were drunks. Others were mentally ill. Still others were cast here by unfortunate circumstance and had become resigned to their lot. As the young man passed them, he knew he could not live with that sort of resignation. But neither did he know how to pull himself up. And so he continued down.

He found himself descending the steps of track twenty-five. The platform was deserted and dim in this off-hour, so no one saw him hop down onto the tracks. Or so he thought. In a moment he was stumbling away from the pitiless world above, into a dark tunnel. He made his way through the blackness, not slowing his pace, and he fell many times, shredding his palms on the railroad ties below. Still, he continued on. He wasn't really sure what he was doing, until the headlights appeared far ahead. They lit the track in front of him and the many other tracks on either side that ran deep under the superstructures of the city. He stopped moving and stood there, staring into the light, until he knew for sure that the train was on his track, zeroing in on him.

If he stood his ground and let the train bear down on him, would anyone ever know? Would anyone ever find him in the mildewed darkness? Or was this the perfect place to disappear for good?

His heart beat a rapid, unnatural rhythm as the ground beneath him rumbled with his approaching end. No horn was blown. Perhaps the conductor wasn't watching the track. Or perhaps he was purposely looking the other way.

As the young man stood there, he wondered whether this would be an act of bravery or cowardice and, realized that, in the end, he did not care; in ten seconds, the answer to the question wouldn't matter.

The blinding headlights filled his entire mind, and he leaned forward to receive them…but then somewhere deep beneath his desire to leave this world, an instinct for survival kicked in and surged powerfully up his spine, sizzling in every nerve ending. The fear became so intense that he screamed louder than the roar of the train, and leaped out of the way. The train caught the heel of a shoe and spun him around, slamming him against one of the many steel I-beams that held up the city above, and he gripped onto that beam as the underdraft threatened to drag him under the train, to those crushing wheels that were suddenly far less attractive than they had been a moment before.

When the train was gone he put his head into his hands and, for the first time in many years, he cried. He wept long and loud, crying for all the things lost in his life, and for all the things that he would never be.

NEAL SHUSTERMAN

It was when he paused for breath that he first heard the rats.

No. Not rats. These skittering sounds were too slow, too heavy to be the footfalls of rats. He looked up and around. While his central vision was still blurred by the bright imprint of the train headlights on his retina, he did see rapidly moving shadows in his peripheral vision. They darted from track to track, hiding behind I-beams. They appeared human.

Finally the shadows stopped before him. He could hear them breathing steadily, just a few feet away, and he began to worry.

He knew of the mole-people: the unloved of the city, who banded together in the city's many tunnels. Some were friendly and accepting of newcomers. Others were dark and dangerous.

"Go away," he snarled at the three figures before him. "I don't have anything to steal."

There was silence for a moment, as if these figures had all the time in the world. Then the one closest to him spoke. "We wish to know your name."

The voice sounded young. A boy's voice, still in the process of changing.

"What do you care?" answered the destitute young man, still clearing the tears from his eyes.

Another moment of silence, and then again the statement, calm and controlled. "We wish to know your name."

The figures before him patiently waited for a response.

"Robert," he finally spat out. "Robert Gunderson."

"We've been watching you, Robert Gunderson," said

another voice, this one female. "We saw you challenge the train and survive."

"I didn't mean to survive," he told them. "I just lost my nerve."

"We know this," said a third voice. Another boy, with a voice much raspier than the other's. "This is why we've made ourselves known."

"Look at us, Robert Gunderson," said the boy in front, clearly the leader of the three. The girl then turned on a flashlight, lighting up their faces in shadow-filled relief. Robert gasped at the sight, because it was far from what he'd expected. He'd expected to see three filthy tunnel-rats, held together by hate and mud-stained rags. But there was nothing dirty about this trio. As he sat there wiping his eyes clear, he began to sense that these were not homeless people who took refuge in tunnels. These kids were something entirely different. Their hair was shaved around their ears, but dense and long everywhere else. It hung down their back and about their shoulders. Their clothes were coarse, woven garments, but on closer inspection Robert could see they were made up of tiny patches sewn together from a thousand different fabrics. Each wore wide metallic wristlets and ankle bracelets with intricate designs, and hand-carved hieroglyphics that looked part English, part something else—Arabic or Russian, or Chinese—or maybe a combination of all three. They wore watches on—of all places—their right ankles. The leader, whose hair flowed in thick bronze locks, wore a shining metallic vest that looked like some sort of ancient chain mail. Robert stared at that vest for the longest time, knowing there was something even stranger about it,

NEAL SHUSTERMAN

and the rest of their metallic accessories, but he couldn't quite say what. Even their flashlight was strange—its face oblong instead of round, and its shaft swirling with red and green patterns. It seemed ancient and almost holy.

"Few Topsiders look upon us and live," said the leader. This wasn't a boast or a threat, but a mere statement of fact.

"Then why do *I* live?" asked Robert.

The leader's face remained solemn. "You don't," he said. Then he reached behind him and he pulled a sword out from a leather patchwork sheath. It wasn't smooth and mirrored like the swords Robert had seen in movies. This was specked and rough—as if it were made of aluminum foil, pounded and re-formed until it was heavy, sharp, and dangerous. And the sword's handle—it seemed to be little more than the grip of a gearshift.

It was then Robert realized what was so strange about the metallic objects they wore. The bracelets were forged of discarded tin cans. The chain-mail vest was a thousand soda-can pop-tops strung together. Everything they had, from their patchwork clothes to their relic of a flashlight, was made out of the world's garbage.

"Today you die, Robert Gunderson," said the leader, and with that he raised his trash-hewn sword above his head and swung it toward Robert's neck in a swift, killing arc.

■ ■ ■

This was Talon's favorite part. But although he felt a thrill rush through him as he brought the blade down, he kept his face hard and unrevealing. Before him the nineteen-year-old man who had been named Robert Gunderson closed his eyes and grimaced, waiting for his head to be lopped off by Talon's blade…but Talon had something else in mind. He stopped his blade just before it touched his skin, then rested the sword heavily on Gunderson's shoulder. The look of surprise and relief on Gunderson's face was a fine thing indeed.

Gutta turned her flashlight in Gunderson's eyes so they could see him—his every move, and the sincerity of his words.

"You have fallen through the bottom of the World," Talon said, his voice a monotone, almost like a chant. "Say it!"

"I…I have fallen through the bottom of the world," repeated Gunderson, his eyes darting back and forth, not understanding—not knowing how important this moment in his life was.

"Do you renounce the Topside? All its joys and evils?" asked Talon, trying to find a depth in his voice that had not yet come. "Do you shed all ties that held you there?"

"What is this?" demanded Gunderson.

"Answer the question," snapped Railborn, his voice raspy and hard, like his father's. Of the three of them, Railborn had the least patience when it came to catching fallers.

Talon, who was leading today's mission, threw his friend a warning look, then turned back to the frightened faller sitting in the dust before them.

"Nothing holds me there," said Gunderson with just the right level of bitterness in his voice to convince Talon that he told the truth.

"Do you swear never to seek the sky again, for as long as you may live?"

Gunderson faltered a bit with this one. Then, as Talon watched, some color came to the lonely faller's face. He seemed to understand, at least in part, what was happening, what was being asked of him—and what he was being offered. His resistance began to fade, and his falling spirit seemed to open for them to catch.

"Yes, I swear," he said. And then again, with even more resolve, "Yes, I swear."

Talon removed the sword from their pledge's shoulder, and slipped it into the sheath his mother had painstakingly sewn for him from a hundred discarded wallets. "Robert Gunderson is dead," Talon announced. "Stand from the dirt, faller."

The man who had been Robert Gunderson stood up, wafting his filthy stench in their direction as they did. His smell was an abomination that would soon be discarded, along with his former self.

"Remove your clothes," said Gutta, who had her own favorite parts of the ritual.

"Why?"

"Just do it," snapped Railborn.

Talon sighed at his friend's impatience. "To come into the Downside," Talon explained, "you can bring nothing from the Topside but your flesh. You will even leave your name behind."

"My name?"

"Fallers don't need names," said Gutta.

Talon took a step closer and put a reassuring arm on the faller's shoulder. "You will be given a new name when you have earned it. For now, you must remove your Topside garments and follow us."

Talon reached over and pushed Gutta's flashlight down so the faller could disrobe in darkness.

"You're no fun," Gutta grumbled at Talon.

When the faller was as bare as the day he had first entered the world, Talon led the way. He could hear the faller's feet squishing through the midworld muck behind him, while Railborn flailed his sword at some stray pigeons that haunted the train tunnel.

They continued on, veering down a tunnel with rails so seldom used that they didn't have the polished sheen of more well-worn tracks. At last they stopped at a soot-blackened cinder block wall that could have been there since the very birth of the city.

"What's wrong?" asked the faller. "Why are we stopping here?"

"Nothing's wrong," Talon answered simply and he motioned to Railborn, the largest of the three. Railborn leaned against the wall, and it gave inward, leaving a large rectangular opening. Gutta turned off her flashlight to reveal the glow of a single gas lamp within the secret passageway. Its flame cast just enough light to show the set of worn stairs beyond, heading down into darkness.

The faller peered in but did not dare move toward the stairwell. He waited for Talon and the others, but they did not go any further.

"The rest of the journey you must make by yourself," Talon told him. "No one can lead you there."

The faller looked apprehensively down the steps, then back at Talon. "No one can lead me *where?*"

"You'll find out," said Gutta.

It was only after the faller had taken the first step into the passageway that Talon told him something to ease his fear. "At the bottom of the steps," said Talon, "you'll find a subway tunnel that hasn't been used for two generations. Walk with the breeze to your back and continue hudward. You'll get there."

Railborn looked at him sharply, for Talon was not supposed to offer anything to the faller but a chance. No kind words. No directions. But it was Talon's call, and this far from home he could do as he pleased.

"Go on before we change our minds," said Gutta.

The faller took a slow step forward, and another. Then finally he descended, disappearing into the hidden shadows below to seek out the second chance that Talon had placed on his shoulder with the slightest touch of his tinfoil sword.

That should have ended a successful evening's work for the trio, but Talon had other ideas—and the others were obliged to follow him, if for no other reason than to keep Talon out of trouble.

Still full of energy from the thrill of the catch, Talon led his friends up to a sidewalk grate. The night was nearing its end, but still, through the grate above their heads, they could see the soles of shoes hurrying past, on their way to whatever things those strange surface folk did. Some stepped into the yellow cars Talon knew to be taxis and were whisked away. Others lingered, enjoying the warm updraft the vent offered them in the cold night. No Topsider ever noticed the three just below their feet, for no one ever thought to look down.

Railborn, gnawing on a mushroom chip he had found in

his hip pouch, grumbled about the faller they had just caught. "He didn't deserve it."

"You always say that," reminded Gutta, grabbing his chip and eating it herself.

Railborn just pulled out another chip and shrugged. "It's always true."

Talon ignored their bickering and kept his eyes turned upward. From where he stood he could see, through the grate, the tops of two tall buildings on the yonkward and batward sides of the street. Their tips seemed almost to touch in the sky above his head, and all around them flakes of snow fell, but none came near the grate—the updraft made sure of that.

"Why are we here?" Gutta asked. "We caught our faller—why can't we go home?"

"Maybe Talon's got his heart set on catching another one tonight," said Railborn with a taunt in his voice. "I actually think Talon *likes* it."

Talon only spared him the slightest glance. "And what if I do?"

Railborn crossed his arms, a gesture that always made his broad shoulders even more imposing. "I never thought you'd be so...soft."

Talon threw him a cool gaze and gently touched the hilt of his sword as a friendly warning for Railborn to watch himself. "You don't like Catching, Railborn, because you're no good at it."

"Catching reeks like sewage," complained Railborn. "I can't wait for our next rotation. Maybe we'll get the Hunt!"

"We won't get the Hunt," said Talon. "In fact, I wouldn't be surprised if we flunked Catching."

Railborn grimaced at the thought. "Why?"

"Because of you," snapped Gutta.

"Wha'd I do?"

"They're never going to let us hunt anything until *you* learn compassion," said Talon. Railborn just grunted and waved the thought off, but then he paced a bit in the small concrete chamber, knowing it to be true.

Talon reached up to touch the grate above his head. It was cold, in spite of the warm updraft. Cold enough for the chill to run down from his fingertips to his wrist. It felt strange and new, and it reminded Talon how much he wished this rotation could last longer than three months. Their first two rotations—Tapping and Mapping—were nowhere near as exhausting as Catching, but unlike those first rotations, Catching was the first task that brought them to the threshold of the Topside. What they had seen during these nights through storm drains and sewer grates had not impressed Railborn and Gutta, but to Talon, every brief hint of surface life was a wonder: from the sooty smell of the air, to the awful ear-wrenching sounds. Once, he had even seen the slim grin of the moon—tales of which he never believed to be real until he actually saw it through a grate. He didn't mind the endless hours observing prospective fallers each night, and he teased himself by imagining that he might someday see the dawn and not go blind.

"It's getting close to daybreak, Talon," said Gutta, a hint of worry in her voice. "We've got to get out of here."

Talon took his eyes from the grate up above and turned to them. The hem of Railborn's garment fluttered with the draft blowing in from the hole behind him.

"Stand over there," Talon told him. "You, too, Gutta—up against the wall."

The two looked at one another, uncertain. When they didn't move, Talon reached out and pushed them gently against the wall. "I said, stand there!"

Still, Railborn resisted, his stance reminding Talon that although Talon might be the oldest of the three, Railborn was the largest.

"I want you to block the air coming in from below," he explained.

Railborn furrowed his dark eyebrows. "But then the Topside air will come down on us. It'll get cold...."

Talon smiled.

Gutta was quick to cooperate once she saw Talon's smile. She positioned herself so as to take up as much room in the opening as possible and pulled Railborn in with her, squeezing against him to fill all the available space. This time it was Railborn's turn to smile. He offered no further resistance, enjoying the moment and trying to hide the sudden redness in his cheeks.

In a moment the cool air dropped over them like a sheet, and then a sudden gust of wind swooped down, kicking up dust and giving them all a harsh taste of winter.

"I don't like it," said Railborn, shrinking away from the cold. "It's...unnatural."

"Why would Topsiders want to live with that cold?" asked Gutta.

NEAL SHUSTERMAN

"Because they're too stupid to know any better," answered Railborn.

But Talon wasn't so quick to pass judgment. Talon thought that if he could feel what the Topsiders felt, he would understand the mystery of why they were what they were. "The Champ says you can't appreciate being warm until you truly know the cold."

Railborn snorted his disapproval. "The Champ says this, The Champ says that—if everything The Champ says is so wise, why don't you just move in with him and spare us from having to hear you talk about him?" But even as Railborn spoke, there was fear in his voice—because he knew, just as Talon did, that The Champ was a force to be reckoned with; a man whose words had profundity none of them would dare challenge.

"If people knew you were talking with him, there'd be trouble," warned Railborn.

"He's not *really* a Topsider," said Gutta.

"Why do you always side with Talon?"

"Quiet!" Talon raised a hand, refusing to listen to Railborn's warnings. Instead, he concentrated on the icy wind swirling around him, filling him with gooseflesh.

The cold was by no means a pleasant sensation—but it wasn't as awful as Railborn made it sound.

Talon waited a moment longer, hoping, and watched the space above the vent. And then what he was waiting for finally came. The snow! The wind above had stopped for a moment, and as soon as it did, thick tufts of the stuff drifted down through the grate, settling on the ground around them and disappearing. Talon focused on a single flake as it wafted down toward him. To Talon the tiny thing was like a messenger from a strange world that lay just out of reach. What an amazing existence this speck of frozen sky had had! Falling from the distant heavens, drifting between sky-piercing towers, just to end its life here before his eyes. Talon held his hand up, and the snowflake landed on the back of his knuckle. He could feel its cold, gentle touch on his skin.

He brought it down to observe it, so gently resting there, already beginning to melt. He wanted so much to keep it— and then realized there was a way that he could. He began to bring the snowflake on the back of his hand toward his mouth.

"Talon, no!" said Gutta. "What if it's poison?!"

"You don't believe those stories, do you?" Then Talon licked the snowflake away, feeling the tiny, almost imperceptible chill as it dissolved on the tip of his tongue.

Gutta and Railborn unwedged themselves from the space they clogged. There were a few moments when the cold and warm air fought each other for control—but finally the cold drained away, and the warm updraft kept the snow away once more.

"What did it taste like?" asked Gutta.

"I don't know," answered Talon. "It didn't taste like anything…but…"

"But what?"

Talon tried to put the feeling into words, but the sensation had passed so quickly, he was already forgetting it. He wished he could have a second taste, but the hour was late and they were expected home. "Let's go—dawn will be coming soon."

"How would you know?" snapped Railborn. "Have you ever seen it?"

"I've heard it's blue," Gutta offered, letting her eyes drift to the grate again and the dark sky beyond. "I've heard that the dawn paints all things a deep royal blue, before the sun comes and burns it away out of anger."

"The sun isn't angry," said Talon. "It just...*is*." Then he turned from the grate and headed down, toward home, hoping that tomorrow night might bring a fresh fall of snow to the tip of his tongue.

High Perimeters

If you tried to find the reasons for the Great Shaft Disaster, and why the events that surrounded it occurred the way they did, you might find yourself wandering in your own Downside maze.

To the Topsiders, it was all a simple matter of incompetent engineering. To the Downsiders, the whole fiasco was punishment for the lawlessness that reigned in these days without a proper leader—the same lawlessness that propelled some of the younger Downsiders to bend and sometimes break the age-old rules that kept the two worlds apart.

And then again, the disaster could have been nothing more than brainless, pointless luck—something that certain cynical observers both above and below would agree upon.

In truth, it was a combination of all three, coupled with the gentlest taste of a single snowflake, and the burning need of a lonely girl.

■ ■ ■

Somewhere near the highest perimeter of Topside life, Lindsay Matthias finally came to the realization of how small and insignificant she was. It was the day after Christmas and, as her mother liked to remind her, the first day of the rest of her life—which she now feared would end in a midair collision, or terrorist bombing, or some other such catastrophic aviation event. She flew to New York twice a year to see her father, but it didn't change the fact that she hated flying alone. In fact, she hated flying period.

She fiddled with the ends of her hair as the plane bounced to and fro. She wore her long blond hair in a single, tight French braid that she liked to drape around her right shoulder like a golden sash. It was nowhere near as magnificent as her mother's braid, which stretched down to the small of her back. "It's a hairstyle that only suits the most attractive, or least attractive girls," her mother once told her, but failed to suggest which of the two Lindsay was. Like so many of her mother's comments, it was maddeningly ambiguous—such as when she would tell Lindsay how beautiful she was "in a certain light," or lovingly say, "You remind me of myself at your age," when she always referred to her own teenage years as awkward and unpleasant. But Lindsay knew she was, at the very least, reasonably attractive, and that was enough for her. Right now, though, she was in danger of breaking out in a case of nervous zits.

"Are the wings supposed to move like that?" she asked the stewardess as their descent into the New York area brought them through a pocket of "mild" turbulence.

The stewardess smiled at her with professional patience. "Of course they are," she said.

"If they didn't flex with the wind, little lady," added the know-it-all passenger beside her, "they'd snap right off like pieces of plywood."

It really wasn't the kind of information she wanted to hear.

"Are you headed home?" the stewardess asked in an undisguised attempt to change the subject.

Lindsay hesitated. "I don't know. I suppose I am."

The truth was, Lindsay was in transit between homes—and not just in the usual transcontinental-divorced-parental sense. This time her ticket was one-way. All of her possessions were crammed into three suitcases somewhere in the hold. Her mother had seen her off at the airport in a hurry because she had her own flight to catch, and in theory, her father was meeting her at LaGuardia. But theories often proved to be unsound—especially where her father was concerned. He was a man who lived his life twenty minutes behind schedule, and in a perpetual state of apology. More than likely it would be her unbrother Todd at the airport, suitably annoyed at having to be there. The thought of being greeted by Todd was more stomach-turning than the turbulence.

"Pretty up here, ain't it," said the know-it-all man beside her, trying to peer out of her window. He wore the Texas twang in his voice like a badge of honor.

"I try not to look," she answered, trying to hide her own Texas accent. She was determined to lose her drawl so she didn't come off like a tourist in New York. *Tourists are tar-*

NEAL SHUSTERMAN

gets, her latest book on personal safety had told her. *Never be a tourist, even when you are.* Well, if nothing else, living in New York would put her self-defense training to use.

"You really should look," nagged the man. "It's one of the great privileges of modern life. A hundred years ago, not a soul on Earth could see what's out your window right now."

Still, Lindsay had no desire to look. It wasn't so much the flying that bothered her. It was the helplessness of being completely within someone else's control—her life entirely out of her hands. She didn't know why that should bother her—after all, she ought to be used to that feeling by now. From the time she was an infant, Lindsay's marching orders were to get with her mother's program. Problem was, the program was constantly changing. Her mother was a career college student, forever chasing a Ph.D. but never quite certain of which one she wanted. This would have been fine had parenting been on her list of personal skills. But poor Mom couldn't even nurture a cactus garden. After years of hopscotching through relationships and time zones, her mom finally decided to run off with her zoology professor to spend three years in Africa, studying the mating habits of white rhinos. And since there were no Girl Scouts or gifted classes on the Serengeti, Mom handed Lindsay over to dear old Dad—this time not just for vacation, but for all eternity.

"Landing at LaGuardia sure is something special," twanged the man beside her. "You come down right over the city. No better view anywhere, especially this time of day."

To get the man off her back, she finally looked out of her window. She thought she would find patchwork farmlands, but they were already above the suburban sprawl that surrounded the city. It was twilight—the sky was full of color, but she didn't look up. She could only look to the ground, where streetlights were already beginning to come on. To Lindsay, it looked like a grid of computer chips, stretching out for miles and miles. *So many people,* she thought. Lindsay could count on a single hand the people who really cared about her. And now, outside her 767 window, was a brutal reminder of how many people didn't.

"Kind of makes you feel real small," said the man beside her. "Puts your life into perspective."

"Yes, it does," said Lindsay, finally understanding what a cruel thing perspective could be.

■ ■ ■

In a place where perspective never reached the horizon, Talon Angler cradled his little sister in his arms. "Tell me about the Topside," asked Pidge in between bouts of coughing. He tried to entertain her with her favorite toy—an old battery-operated puppy that had lost most of its fur long before it came to the Downside. But she had had no interest in any of her toys since her sickness had come. Now, as Talon touched his lips to her forehead to feel her fever, he could tell it was soaring.

"Please, Talon," she asked again.

Talon took a deep breath. "The Topside is an Inside-out, Downside-up kind of place," he told her. "Filled with strange people and strange machines."

"Tell me about the people," Pidge rasped out. Talon shifted position, trying to remember the Topside lore he had gathered from his brief glimpses through the grates, the old tales, and, of course, the strange ramblings of The Champ. All considered, Talon knew very little, but ever since he began his Catching rotation, little Pidge saw him as the world's foremost authority on surface life.

"The people's minds have been scorched by the sun," Talon continued, "until they can't tell up from down. That's why they build towers instead of tunnels, like normal people."

Pidge ran her feverish hand along Talon's handcrafted pop-top vest, making a gentle metallic rattle with her fingers. "What are the towers for?"

"Punishment," explained Talon. "All day long Topsiders hurry from one tower to another, in uncomfortable shoes. They race around in a circle from avenue to avenue, getting some money each time they go around, then giving it right back to the rich people, who own the streets."

Pidge coughed again as Mom slipped through the curtain to bring her a bowl of throgsneck soup, just like Grandma used to make. "Nothing a nice bowl of throgsneck soup can't cure," Mom said. But that was just wishful thinking. Pidge's cough was a thick liquid bark, and it would take more than soup to make it go away. So far none of the usual remedies were working. There were whispers that it might be a return of the dreaded Tunnel Fever—but then, that's what they called any sickness that killed people. Talon doubted there really was such a thing.

Their mom began to fuss with Pidge, feeling her forehead, fluffing her pillow, and Pidge, in no mood for parental doting, pushed her mother's hand away and began to whine.

"It's okay, Mom," said Talon, who was always best with Pidge when she was ill, "I'll stay with her."

J
C-1

His mother threw Talon a worried glance as she gently set the soup down before them. "See if you can get her to eat," she said, then reluctantly slipped back out through the heavy curtains.

Pidge looked at the rich, flavorful brew, but had no interest in it. "Tell me about the machines."

"You know about those," said Talon.

"Tell me anyway."

"Okay…there are the trains, which the smarter Topsiders use, that take them underground. Then there are the Topside cars—loud, sludge-smelling things that start and stop, start and stop, and never get anywhere. The cars have loud horns that the Topsiders blow at one another to keep each other awake while they sit in their cars, waiting to move."

Pidge laughed, but it came out as a pained cackle. "Are there any good-guys up there, or are they all bad-guys?"

"I'm not sure," said Talon. "But I do know that there's a place called jail, where the bad ones go."

"I've heard of that place," whispered Pidge. "Do all Topsiders go there?"

"They all do sooner or later," Talon explained. "And they have to stay there a long time if they don't have a special card that gets them out of jail for free."

Pidge looked away. "I feel sorry for them," she said. "Maybe we could build enough tunnels so they could all come down here, and we could teach them up from down."

"Maybe," whispered Talon. Pidge's eyelids were drooping. Before she slipped off to sleep, he tried to bring a spoonful of soup to her lips, but she pushed it away with a limp hand. Then in a moment she was asleep, rasping slow breaths.

■ ■ ■

Throughout his Catching expedition that night, Talon carried the unrelenting feel of Pidge's fever against his lips. Gutta, and even Railborn, could tell that Talon was not his usual self. As they peered through the narrow drain slits and concrete cracks to track potential fallers, Talon's mind seemed elsewhere. Because they knew about Pidge's condition, neither was surprised when Talon brought up the idea of a Topside Raid.

"No! Don't even *think* about it," bellowed Railborn loud enough to be heard through the exhaust vent they stood behind, watching a dirty man with a shopping cart.

"It's been years since the last official raid—maybe it's time."

Railborn had already begun to pace. "What makes you think anyone's gonna listen to you? And, anyway, why would anyone go after what happened the last time?"

"No one really knows what happened the last time!" Talon reminded him. All anyone knew for sure was that twelve strong Downside men were sent up one fall, wrapped in heavy skins from head to toe and wearing dark goggles to protect them from the unpredictable effects of the sun— then, a few hours later, they came back battered and bloody. According to their mad ravings, the moment they rose from the manhole they had been trampled by what they described as "a frenzied stampede of crazed Topsiders"— thousands of them running in an endless pack down First Avenue, each wearing short pants, and numbers on their backs. Needless to say, no one believed them, and they were all locked away in the Chamber of Soft Walls—victims, they say, of Sun Dementia. It was a dark moment in Downside history that no one liked to talk about.

"Well, then, what about an *unofficial* raid? A secret one—just us three. We'll go after nightfall and come back before dawn."

Talon turned to Gutta for support, but she was not forthcoming. Instead, she leaned back with her arms folded, reserving judgment as she watched the two boys debate.

"It's against the law!" said Railborn. "I don't know about you, but I don't want to end up on a slime gang, cleaning tunnel walls all my life."

"That won't happen—people go on secret night raids all the time, right, Gutta?"

Gutta still stood with her arms folded. "I've heard rumors…"

"Made-up stories!"

"Oh yeah?" said Talon, getting in Railborn's face. "Where do you think lightbulbs come from, Railborn? And batteries, and pens, and conditioning shampoo?"

"Topsiders make them for us, like bees make honey," was Railborn's rote response.

"Yeah, they make them—but how does it all get here? Do you think the rain just washes it down the drains to us? Think about it, Railborn. *Somebody has to get it!* It's just that no one talks about it."

Talon's logic struck a chord in Railborn, but it only served to make him even more obstinate. "If no one talks about it, then it's not my problem. It's like my father says—"

"Your *father?*" Talon laughed, tossing a glance down at

NEAL SHUSTERMAN

Railborn's alligator boots. "I wouldn't put too much faith in a man who hunts an entire species to death!"

At that, Railborn pulled out his sword and swung it against the wall. His ruddy face turned a deep shade of crimson. "That wasn't his fault," growled Railborn. "And if you say one more thing about my father, I swear I'll sludge-face you, Talon. I'll sludge-face you in the main line!"

Finally Gutta came between them. "Now that's something I'd like to see," she said with a smile, pushing them away from one another with arms that were deceptively strong for their size. "But I'd rather not see it now."

Both Talon and Railborn kept their silence for a moment. Beyond the grate, a car horn was suddenly silenced by a crunch of metal, followed by angry, incomprehensible voices. Two taxis had collided. It seemed to be what they did best. Talon paid it no mind. Instead, he told his friends what was really on his mind.

"My sister needs medicine."

Railborn offered him an impotent shrug. "How do you know they have what she needs?"

Railborn had a point—Talon didn't know—but he *had* heard rumors about people who were brought back from the edge of death by Topside potions in orange vials. Topsiders might not be too bright, but there were certain things they did very well. It was no secret that battling death was one of those things.

"She'll get better," offered Railborn, gripping Talon's shoulder in a rare show of compassion. "I'm sure she will."

"And if she doesn't?"

Railborn pursed his lips and spoke gently. "Then it just wasn't meant to be…and none of the medicine in the world could change that."

Not able to hold each other's gaze, they turned to peer out of the grate. The two cars, their hoods spewing steam, clogged up traffic like a rat in a drain. Right now none of the three were interested in the mysteries and miseries of the Topside streets. While they had been arguing, their potential faller had taken his shopping cart and moved on. There was nothing keeping them here anymore, and it was time to make the trek home.

As they wound their way through air ducts and forgotten subbasements, Talon could not get the image of his sick sister out of his mind. "A true friend would come to the surface with me, if I asked," he told Railborn.

"But a true friend would never ask another to break the law," was Railborn's response.

Railborn went on ahead, but Gutta lingered with Talon, waiting until Railborn was out of earshot. "I'd go with you, Talon," she said, "if you asked me."

Talon smiled at her offer but knew that Railborn was right: A true friend would never ask. Besides, what good was a Topside Raid when he wasn't even sure what he was looking for? He thanked Gutta and told her to go on ahead.

"Maybe you can talk to The Champ," she suggested. "He'll know what to do. He might even get you what you need. I think that maybe he has his own magic."

"Yeah, maybe." The last thing he wanted to do was beg The Champ for charity, but now it seemed he had little choice.

Talon sat down on the rusted remains of some disowned

appliance, then watched as Gutta disappeared behind Railborn down a jagged hole in a concrete floor to an
abandoned utility tunnel below. When they were gone,
Talon took a different route, trying to lose himself in the
maze of subbasements and accessways that made up the
uppermost reaches of the Downside's High Perimeter.
Places that rested so tantalizingly close to the surface, you
could feel the air around you change with the weather.

As frustrating as it was, Talon had to admire the way
Railborn stuck to his sword and held firm to the laws and
edicts that governed Downside life. A few years ago, no one
would have dreamed of traveling to the surface without getting permission from the proper authority. The problem
was, no such authority existed now. There hadn't been a real
leader—a "Most-Beloved"—since before Talon was born,
because the Downsiders thoroughly believed that it was better to have no leader than a bad one. These days everyone
was waiting for the perfect someone who would be sponta-
neously and unanimously exalted into the lifelong position.
Unfortunately, nobody was universally loved anymore.
There were the Wise Advisors, of course, but without a
leader to run things, no one really listened to what the Wise
Advisors had to say—mainly because nothing they ever said
was either wise or advisable.

Talon pondered and puzzled over his alternatives as he
wandered the many passageways of the High Perimeter, still
not ready to cross the clearly marked boundaries that separated Downside chambers from those of the upper world. It
was as he wandered that fate—and the answer to his woes—
hit him like a brick.

In a city where things were constantly being torn down to build a bigger and better tomorrow, falling bricks were more the rule than the exception. Demolition was a growth industry, and the buildings that remained were endlessly renovated to satisfy the ever-changing tastes and lifestyles of those who lived there.

On East Eighty-fourth Street, one such home was under renovation—or, to be more precise—*two* such homes. Two identical three-story brownstone town houses were being merged into one. And all because Lindsay Matthias had moved in with her father.

It had begun as a simple enough project: rip out a living-room wall and some upstairs walls, then join the two buildings like Siamese twins. A single living space with two faces on Eighty-fourth Street. But things are never as easy as they seem, and Lindsay Matthias found herself living in a home that was perpetually incomplete.

Right now, the second-floor hallway was the center of incompletion. In the middle of the hallway, where there had once been a mirror, was now a jagged hole lined with broken plaster and brick. Beyond that hole was the matching hallway of the building next door. It was an eerie thing to see because it gave the illusion that the mirror was still there. Lindsay had been tempted to step through the looking glass but didn't dare because there was a two-foot gap between the buildings that didn't show on the blueprints— hence the trouble with remodeling—and beneath that gap was a pitch-black drop down to who-knew-where. That hole in the wall had been there ever since she had arrived from Texas the week before, and since her room was closest to it, she found the winter nights bitterly cold.

"That's life in the big city," Todd, her preening weasel of a stepbrother, had said. "Deal with it, or die." Todd probably missed the mirror more than anyone else because it gave him one more opportunity to admire that pretty face of his that all the girls fell for. That is, all the girls too stupid to figure out what a preening weasel Todd was.

If there was any saving grace for Lindsay, it was that she didn't actually share any genetic material with Todd. How she and Todd ended up under the same roof was a story in and of itself. It was Dad's fault, really, because he had a tendency to fall for flighty, impulsive women who never quite took to motherhood.

Todd's story wasn't much better than Lindsay's. His mother was a dancer who gave birth to Todd long before she even met Dad. Then, shortly after she and Dad were married, during her Sunday matinee performance of *Cats*, the woman took a bad leap, plunging right into the orchestra pit. This was one cat who didn't land on her feet. They rushed her off to the hospital while Todd, only eight years old at the time, was left in tears, clutching her dismembered tail in the theater lobby.

During her three months in traction she had a spiritual awakening, and upon her discharge from the hospital she joined a cult in the mysterious recesses of Brooklyn, where she remained ever after. Dad, his heart being much larger than his brain, became Todd's guardian, and lavished on the boy all it took to spoil him putrid. None of this, of course, explained Todd's cruel streak and his atrophied conscience. He was the kind of kid who wouldn't just pull the wings off of flies; he would then dangle the severed wings in front of the flightless insects just to torment them.

In spite of having come from similar domestic fall-outs, Lindsay was quite different. Having spent her formative years in the company of academics, she had a love of literature and art. She could explore the city's libraries and museums for weeks on end, and suspected she would do precisely that, because Dad wasn't exactly bending over backwards to spend time with her. Mark Matthias was too emotionally involved with civil engineering to have a life beyond his work. But then, it takes a special kind of man to devote his life to the building of an aqueduct.

Dad's late hours left plenty of time for Lindsay and Todd to share—and since the moment Lindsay's plane touched down, she had become a new wingless fly for Todd to torment.

It was 10:00 in the evening when Todd burst into Lindsay's room without knocking, as he always did. "Lindsay, Lindsay, Lindsay…" he said with a sigh and a sad shake of his head. "You and I need to talk."

"Why?" she asked apprehensively, putting down the book she was reading and pulling her knees up under her covers.

He sat at her desk chair and used her bed as a footrest for his grimy shoes. "You just had to run and tell Dad I was smoking, didn't you?"

"I didn't run to him. *He* asked *me* about it."

Todd grabbed a paper clip from the desk and used it to scrape the dirt out from under his fingernails. "There's a little thing called a 'white lie,' you know."

"I won't lie to my father."

"*Our* father," insisted Todd.

"If you say so."

Todd put down the paper clip and leaned in closer. "He lectured me for forty-five minutes," he said. "That's a new record."

But obviously none of it sank in, because Todd's breath reeked like a diesel exhaust pipe.

"Listen, Todd. The last thing I want is to stand between you and a premature death, so suck cigarettes all you want, but I won't lie to Dad about it."

"You don't get it, do you?" said Todd—which was something he often said. Lindsay had yet to figure out what "it" she was supposed to "get." Todd glanced down at the nightstand, and Lindsay reacted an instant too late. His lanky arm snapped out like a toad's tongue and snatched up her book before she could stop him.

"So, what ya' reading?" He closed the book to look at the cover, losing her place. "*The Time Machine*?"

"I happen to like H. G. Wells," she said, trying to sound far less defensive than she did.

"Yeah," scoffed Todd. "So do most people who don't have a life."

He stood and sauntered toward the door, book still in hand. Lindsay swung out of bed to go after him. "Give me the book, Todd."

He didn't turn back to her until he reached the threshold. When he did, he put out his hand to keep her at arm's length as she grabbed for the book that he still held teasingly out of reach.

"I've got some advice for you, Lindsay. It's ten o'clock on a Friday night. Most people are getting ready to party, and you're sitting here in bed. Do yourself a favor. You're in New York now. Get a life."

And with that he hurled the book toward the jagged hole in the unfinished hallway. The book hit a loose brick, knocking it free, and both brick and book disappeared down the dark crevice between the twin brownstone buildings.

"Cool," said Todd. "Two points!" And he sauntered away.

"Todd!" screamed Lindsay, grinding her teeth in fury, but it was no use. She heard the front door open and close, and he was gone.

So angry was she that she didn't hear the distant yowl a few seconds after the book and the brick had fallen....

...But much later that night, she did dream she saw something.

She dreamed that she got up in the middle of the night to get a glass of water. And on her way back to her room, she saw a face watching her from the gap that separated the two buildings. Curly-haired, and with large-pupiled eyes, the shadow-boy peered at her from the dark gap, like a ghost staring out through the looking glass. Then he disappeared with a tiny clatter to that dark space between the bricks. It wasn't until the morning, when Lindsay found the glass of water on her nightstand, that she realized she hadn't been dreaming at all.

3

The Champ

On a sorry patch of land on 115th Street, where the roar of the congested FDR Drive actually stunted the growth of trees, sat a small, untended park. It was the kind of park where kids shot baskets through broken chain-netted hoops—kids who had to be skilled at avoiding the clumps of weeds that grew through every wrinkle in the aging asphalt. Twenty yards from the dilapidated court rested a brick building that contained a municipal pool. The pool had been long condemned, but was so forgotten by the Department of Parks and Recreation that no one had ever gotten around to demolishing it.

The front door was sealed by a rusted knot of a chain and a massive padlock that wasn't opening for all the keys in the world. As for the windows, they were barred and boarded over, allowing no light to get in. Had there not been a back door, the place might have remained deserted until it grew old enough to be deemed a landmark. But there *was* a back door, and that door had no padlock—which made the pool building ripe for occupation. In fact, in a city where one had to be a student of the obituaries to find an apartment, what made it odd was that only *one* person had set up house in there, and not an entire colony.

The seventy-eight-year-old man who lived in the shell of the abandoned pool was born Reginald Champlain, but the few who knew him just called him "The Champ." He was wizened by many years of hard living, and had learned the art of living in style. His life story, colorful and intriguing though it may be, is important here only inasmuch as it led him to this particular place at this particular time.

This wayward park was built on the remnants of the 1894 City Fair, and the pool itself was built directly over the dry riverbed of the fair's Tunnel of Love. While love was not eternal, apparently its tunnel was, because it had become a part of the Downside—and the deep end of the waterless pool, a good twenty feet deep, provided a fine interface between the world above and the world below.

Trying to ignore the throbbing knot on his head, Talon made his way past several ancient decaying swan boats until reaching a spot where the dirt ceiling gave way to a broken drainpipe and a square drain above it, eighteen inches wide. Technically speaking, the pool was Topside territory, but with no windows and no real Topside visitors, it could be argued that the lonely building was part of the Downside's High Perimeter and not part of the Topside at all. At any rate, it was convenient for Talon to consider it such.

"I thought I heard you scraping around down there," said

NEAL SHUSTERMAN

The Champ as he saw Talon pulling himself up through the drain. "What are you doin' out and about so early, hmm?"

Early for Talon was just after dark. Usually when he popped by for a visit with The Champ, it was in the wee hours of the morning, just before dawn, after a night of Catching.

"Thought I'd surprise you."

"Now why would a kid crawling out of a drain surprise me?"

Talon grinned, but even that grin was hard, for it made the knot on his head ache—a knot he had earned the night before by standing in precisely the wrong place at the wrong time when a Topsider had decided to hurl a brick his way. It had rendered him unconscious for the better part of an hour, and yet he still wasn't sure whether that painful encounter had been bad fortune or good.

The Champ held out his rough hand and helped Talon out of the drain. "Thought you wouldn't come round here anymore after I whomped your behind in our last game." He laughed, and Talon had to smile. Though he was here on urgent business tonight, he still couldn't help but catch a bit of The Champ's contagious laughter.

The Champ was the first wayward Topsider that Talon and his friends had tried to bring into the Downside when their catching rotation first began—and yes, he was more than surprised when the three of them came out of the drain. He had tried to swat them away with a broom—half-convinced they were some sort of hallucination—until finally they made him understand why they had come and what they were offering.

But it turned out they had chosen their first "faller" poorly, for The Champ was content to stay exactly where he was. It was The Champ's face that first caught Talon's attention. The whitest of beards across the darkest of faces. His skin was a deep chocolate, and although there were a fair number of dark-skinned people in the Downside, somehow The Champ seemed different. Talon himself had a great-grandfather with chocolate skin—but by the time it distilled down to Talon, the richness had bleached out into the pale hue of his mother's side of the family. Perhaps it was the resemblance to his great-grandfather that endeared The Champ to Talon, and kept Talon coming back long after he realized the old man would never be drawn to their world.

Or perhaps it was the way the man had chosen to live his life that impressed Talon: the way he needed neither the Topside nor Downside. The Champ was a man who belonged to neither world—he had created a world all his own here in the shell of the old pool. One needed only to look around to see how well-crafted and self-sufficient The Champ's life was. The walls of his world were the sides of the pool shell, more spacious than most homes, with a dramatic, vaulted ceiling. The sides of the pool had been painted a gunmetal gray by The Champ himself. "Like the *Arizona*," he had once told Talon. "I once served on that ship, you know. Watched from shore as it went down in Pearl Harbor. No sight as awful as the start of a war." Talon had no idea what he was talking about, but it all sounded important and impressive.

There was furniture in The Champ's well-appointed lair:

NEAL SHUSTERMAN

three comfortable sofas, a loveseat, a dining set, and even a chandelier that The Champ had hung from one of the rusty pipes high above. Only the bedroom was spartan—a simple iron bed frame, covered by a taut military blanket, which sat alone in a corner of the deep end.

The legs of all the furniture, of course, had to be carefully sawed to compensate for the slant of the pool bottom, but The Champ had done the job well. In the end, the decor was so effective, it made one wonder why all homes weren't built on such an attractive slant.

And then there were the shelves; dozens of them drilled into the steel side of the pool. Many held knickknacks and cans of food, but there was one special shelving unit where The Champ kept his most valuable collection: his games. As soon as Talon was out of the drain, The Champ went over to that set of special shelves and stood on a chair. "What'll it be today?" he asked.

"The usual," said Talon.

The Champ reached up and carefully pulled out a flat, old box, then set it down on the dining table. "You gonna be the shoe today, or the thimble?"

"I'll be the car," answered Talon.

The Champ opened up the board and they began, but Talon's mind was elsewhere. He moved his piece absently around the board, thinking of weighty decisions he would soon have to make if he were to have any chance of saving his sister's life. As he thought about her wasting away, he felt the awful weight of his own helplessness. It made him feel weak in the elbows and knees—and weaker still that he had to ask someone on the outside for help.

"Marvin Gardens," declared The Champ. "Aren't you going to buy it?"

Talon gave him the money, and The Champ gave him the card. He held it in his hand, looking at it so he didn't have to look at the old man as he spoke. "What do you know about cheating death?"

The Champ rolled his dice and bought Reading Railroad. "Only that it can't be done. In the end, everyone takes the dirt nap."

"Dirt nap?"

"You know," said The Champ, "the deep six; daisy detail; siesta del soil?"

"Oh. Oh, I get it," said Talon, taking his turn. "Kind of backwards, though, isn't it? I mean, going underground *after* you're dead."

That gave The Champ pause for thought. He held the dice, but didn't throw them. "Why? What do your people do…if you don't mind me asking."

Talon minded, but he tried not to let it show. "When someone dies, we divert water from a water main and into a dry runoff tunnel," he explained. "The surge carries them into the world beyond."

"So you just flush 'em," said The Champ, letting out something between a groan and a chuckle. "You flush 'em like a goldfish!"

Suddenly Talon looked up from the board, remembering something. He stood abruptly. "I'll be back."

Talon slipped down the drain, shoved a wet, newspaper-wrapped object under his arm, and climbed back up.

"What's this now?" The Champ asked.

Talon slapped his package down next to the Monopoly board and pulled back the wet pieces of newspaper to reveal a prize carp, as fresh as they come. "My father's a fisherman," Talon explained. "We get these all the time." It was a good foot-and-a-half long, with perfect gold scales that glistened in the light of the hanging chandelier.

"You brought me a giant dead goldfish?"

"It's a carp," explained Talon. "I mean, sure, they start off as goldfish. Topsiders send 'em down into the sewers thinking they're dead—but lots of times they revive. They can live for years down there before we fish them out. Life in the main line makes them real hardy."

The Champ nodded, never taking his eyes off of the fish. "Guess you could call it carpal tunnel syndrome," he said, and laughed aloud at his own joke.

"Anyway," said Talon, "once we catch them, we keep them alive in a freshwater pen for a few months, to get all the sludge out of their system so they're good to eat."

Then The Champ got serious for a moment. "I'll be damned," he murmured. "You wanna talk to someone about cheating death, talk to this here fish." He brushed his fingers across the smooth body of the carp. "It's a shame after all he's been through that he has to end up like this."

Then he turned his eyes to Talon and offered him a grateful nod. "Thank you, Talon. I'll cook it up straightaway. Been a long time since I had a good piece of fish."

Talon looked to the game board again, but the dice seemed to have disappeared. His little silver car now rested on the big question mark labeled CHANCE? and when Talon looked up, he caught The Champ staring at him.

"Why the gift, son? What is it you want from me?"

Talon had to wrestle his own eyes to keep them from looking away. "My sister's very sick," he finally told him, at last baring his helplessness to the old man. "She's got a fever, and won't stop coughing, and I don't know what to do—but if I don't do something, she'll die."

"I'm not a doctor. You have to get her to a hospital."

Talon shook his head. There were some Downside rules even Talon would not break.

The Champ stood up and paced to the shallow end, then he turned to face Talon again. "So what do you want me to do? You think just because we got stars up here we can wish on 'em and make everything better? You think we got magic potions up here?"

Talon stood from the table and cleared his throat. "Yes. I do."

Slowly The Champ made his way back to the deep end. His voice softened as he came down from his higher ground. "You folks want to have your cake and eat it, too, don't you? Hating the Surface until there's something you need."

Talon didn't answer him. He only looked around at the strange spoils The Champ had scavenged from the Topside. In the end, The Champ was no different, and he knew it. Talon waited to see what he would do.

"She's got a fever, you say?"

Talon nodded.

"Coughing up that green stuff?"

Talon nodded again.

The Champ sighed, then gave in. He found a pen, then

flipped a pink five-dollar bill over and began to scribble on the back. "Like I said, I'm no doctor, and I can't be sure what your sister has, but chances are if it can be fixed, one of these'll do it."

He handed the paper to Talon, who tried to read the names. They sounded suitably mystical. Amoxicillin… cephalexin…Augmentin… "Where can I find them?"

"Pharmacy, but you'll never get it without a prescription…."

Talon glanced at the paper again, not quite understanding.

The Champ brushed a worried hand through his thinning hair. "Listen," he said, "sometimes people have the stuff just lying around, you know?" But then he shook his head, angry that he had even suggested it. "The thing is, you're never supposed to take other people's medicine. It's dangerous. You get the wrong stuff, or take too much, or if you're allergic, it can kill you quick as any disease. That's why there're laws against it—you see what I'm saying?"

"I understand," said Talon, accepting this mantle of responsibility. Then, rather than lingering, he thanked The Champ and slipped back into the drain.

"You take care now," said the old man with genuine concern. Talon nodded a stoic good-bye and, in a few short moments he was gone, running through the old Tunnel of Love with a plan already beginning to take shape in his mind.

Party Uptown

Legendary throughout the known world was the great city's celebration of the new year. On the last eve of every year, hundreds of thousands gathered to be part of the festivities in a place appropriately named Times Square, waiting for a ball of light to slip down its pole and herald in a new beginning to the same old story.

People would cheer, throw confetti, and then go about breaking the resolutions they had made only moments before.

The Downside knew of this great celebration, for they, too, marked their days by the same basic calendar and had their own revelry to usher in the year. They would gather in the Brass Junction and the Floodgate Concourse, raising toasts to the days ahead and those gone by. And if you asked, they would be quick to tell you that they were the ones who invented New Year's Eve.

Talon was conspicuously absent from the Downside celebration, and as the midnight hour approached, Railborn and Gutta were concerned.

"New Year's is always his favorite," Railborn anxiously reminded Gutta. "And he always spends it with us...."

"He's probably with Pidge," yelled Gutta, over the echoing roar of the crowds within the cavernous Floodgate Concourse. Surely Talon's parents were both at home tending to their sick daughter, but Talon? Stay home on New Year's Eve?

"Yes," said Railborn. "That must be where he is." But neither of them believed it for an instant.

Meanwhile, several layers of city sediment above them, Todd Matthias was hosting a party. To him, the mania of Times Square was as passé as frozen yogurt and grungewear. He had been there, done that, and was determined to celebrate the new year with others who were equally pompous. He chose to populate his party with choice friends from Icharus Academy, the private school that he, and now Lindsay, attended.

Their father was off at his own New Year's Eve gala—a big affair for VIPs of urban planning. Naturally he had no clue that Todd's "intimate gathering of friends" was actually a cauldron of hormones and questionable fruit punch—a prelude to the all-night bashes that would someday fill Todd's entire college career. In effect, this was a fraternity party with training wheels.

As Lindsay could have predicted, Todd had made no attempt to invite anyone her age. Most of the guests were tenth grade and up because Todd, a freshman, was perpetually brownnosing his way into the older crowd. The only fourteen-year-old girls present beside Lindsay had tagged along with their older boyfriends and were too aloof to have anything to do with her.

As for Todd, he fancied himself the life of the party and probably figured all activity ceased when he left a room. Lindsay watched as he bragged to a gaggle of debutantes, and she silently wished she had a nice hat pin to pop his swelled head.

"Yes, we own both these homes," he bragged, indicating the wide threshold where new masonry now connected the two living rooms. "We decided to expand right here rather than buy that beach house in the Hamptons."

But the joke, as Todd well knew, was that Dad was not a rich man at all. He just knew the right people and had an awful lot of leverage. In truth, he was in debt about as deep as that aqueduct shaft he was digging downtown. If something ever went wrong and the banks called in all the loans, the next sound you would hear would be the Matthias's lives being sucked into a black hole.

But still Todd bragged—because to him it didn't matter whether or not you were rich as long as everyone *thought* you were.

Lindsay moved through the party, wandering around the connected living rooms of the twin town houses, doing her best to feel at home. She did enjoy people-watching—and there were certainly some interesting people to watch. Some had multicolored hair, and others had hair flat and black, dyed to match their nails and lipstick. Some girls dressed in Madison Avenue fashions, while others looked

NEAL SHUSTERMAN

postapocalyptic. Lindsay seemed to be the only one present who wasn't trying to make some glaring fashion statement, and that, oddly, made her different and exotic enough to earn her more than her share of dances. She had to admit she was flattered, and she was more than happy to dance in full view of the malnourished and overaccessorized girls who watched in frustration from the sidelines.

There were some boys who even vied for her attention off the dance floor—but once they started to talk, any interest on Lindsay's part dissolved. One boy, for instance, was only interested in conversation as long as it was about himself. Another had a nervous tic and a strange preoccupation with horses, and a third did nothing but press Lindsay for deep personal information about Todd.

It was right around the time that Todd was entertaining some friends with impersonations that Lindsay decided to make her exit—but something she heard stopped her.

"I'm meeting the water needs of this city for the new millennium," Todd said in an annoyingly accurate imitation of their father. "Five hundred years from now, they'll still be drinking water that came through my aqueduct!"

Todd had one finger extended Heavenward in pontification posture, and the other hand swatted his nose the way Dad did when his allergies bothered him. Even the ones who didn't know Dad laughed, and it made Lindsay furious.

"You're not funny, Todd," she shouted, abruptly ending the laughter and gaining enough attention to quiet down the room.

"You're the only one who thinks so, Pseudo-sis." He

laughed again, hoping to get his friends to chuckle at his nickname for her, but no one did.

"Dad works hard, and his work is important to him. You have no right to make fun of it."

Todd only shrugged it off. "It's just a stupid tunnel."

There was a tense silence between them that could have gotten worse, but everyone's attention shifted when a girl across the room confused some leftover plumber's putty with clam dip and spread herself a Ritz cracker nasty. She began to gag in no uncertain terms, and since it was dangerously close to the punch bowl, everyone came running. The commotion afforded Lindsay a moment to slip away, up to her room.

As she climbed the stairs, leaving behind Todd and his self-absorbed friends, a cold current of air flowed past her down the stairs. Perhaps it was that breeze that made her neck hairs bristle and her steps hesitate. Something wasn't quite right, and it made her uneasy.

When she arrived at her door, she was annoyed to discover that the sanctity of her bedroom had been violated. There, sitting on her bed, was a couple who had decided this was a nice little make-out spot.

"The kissing booth is closed," Lindsay announced. "Make your lip-sandwiches elsewhere."

The couple quickly departed, leaving behind a cloying stench of cologne that could set off the smoke detectors. Honestly, what had she done to deserve this? Lindsay went to her door and began pumping it open and closed to fan away the stench—and that's when she noticed the cold breeze again, coming, as it always did, from the hole in the hallway, the gap between the two buildings. As usual, the thin veil of plastic that was supposed to cover the hole had fallen down to reveal that strange looking-glass image of the building next door. She began to feel uneasy again, and this time she knew why. She had felt that same cold breeze in the middle of the night when she saw—or *thought* she saw—a face peering out at her from the gap. The memory had been so dreamlike, she wasn't exactly sure what had happened, and in the morning things seemed so normal in the light of day that she chose not to think about it. Until now.

On the ground, the piece of black plastic that was supposed to cover the jagged brick hole fluttered and crackled with the air that flowed through the gap from the sky above. But it wasn't just air coming from above, was it?

Lindsay quickly retrieved the pocket flashlight in the bathroom junk drawer, then she made her way to the gap. First she put her hand into the space between the buildings, palm down. The back of her hand was chilled by cold air dropping from above…but her palm became warm, heated by air rising from below. But from where?

She turned on the flashlight and peered down. She saw the new masonry that connected the twin living rooms on the first floor, but directly beneath her there was nothing. The brickwork seemed to descend to the basement foundation, and beneath that was darkness. A sudden shuffling sound behind her made her flinch, and she lost the flashlight. It tumbled into the hole, its light spinning wildly into oblivion. She spun around, but there was no one behind her. She listened again, but could hear nothing beyond the ghostly echoes of the chattering partyers one flight down.

What if there were rats down there? What if they were climbing their way into the house through that gap?

It's just your imagination, Lindsay told herself. Although her imagination had always served her well in times of need, it also had its neurotic little moments, making nonexistent mountains out of imaginary molehills.

She tried to shake off the shivers, telling herself that she had no reason to be concerned...until she noticed the dusty footprints on the hardwood floor. There were only three of them. The first and dustiest was right by the hole in the wall, the second was less pronounced, and the third was barely visible at all.

Well, so what? There are a dozen logical explanations, shouted her rational mind. Maybe it was from one of the workers remodeling the home...or maybe from a party-goer who jumped from one building to the other, over the gap. Or maybe it was some deranged serial killer—after all, Rikers Island was just a hop, skip, and a jump over the East River. They kept the worst criminals there. What if one of them tunneled their way out, and—

"Stop it, Lindsay," she said aloud, hoping that the sound of her own voice might snap some sense into her. And in fact it did. She took a deep breath, and then another, then she took the black plastic tarp off the floor and hung it back on the hooks above the hole—if not sealing it, at least hiding it from view.

She returned to her room, determined to watch the ball come down in Times Square on her TV rather than share the moment with Todd. With her door closed, the small television became the only light in the room, casting shifting blue

NEAL SHUSTERMAN

shadows in every corner, and she took to rebraiding her hair. She carefully unwound the heavy rope of her single French braid, then pulled her thick blond locks over one another, stretching them across her knuckles tighter and tighter. She was not satisfied until she could feel the familiar pull of the braid against her scalp so tight it was almost painful—every strand tightly woven and bound, in perfect control.

As she finished the braid, she noticed a strange smell in the air. It was masked by that sickly-sweet cologne stench still lingering in the room, but as that perfumy odor faded, Lindsay began to catch something beneath it. Something earthy—but not unpleasant. Something clean and crisp, like the smell of the ground in the first moments of a rainstorm. It hit her all at once that there was someone else in the room with her, and this time there was nothing imaginary about it.

She gasped and leaped across the room just as she heard the closet door creak open. The television cast its harsh glow on a figure lunging for her. She screamed, eluding his grasp, and snapped on the light.

This was not one of Todd's guests.

Not even the strangest of Todd's friends wore clothes of this nature, and Lindsay immediately flashed to all of those warnings from her mother before she had skipped off to Africa. She had cautioned Lindsay about the many dangers of New York, as if Lindsay were the one heading into a perilous jungle, and not her.

"Don't!" insisted the boy as he moved toward her again. "Don't scream!" He clasped his hand around her mouth to quiet her, but she was ready for him. She had trained and prepared for this moment for years. She grabbed his wrist, turning his own momentum into a weapon against him, tugged down on it just so, and he flipped over, landing hard on his back with a thud and a groan. Then, as he tried to scramble to his feet, Lindsay thrust her hand into the various toiletries on her dresser. She knocked over several bottles before closing her hands around a cold black little canister. She spun on her strange, earthen-smelling assailant as he rose from the floor and quickly emptied the can of pepper spray into the boy's wide-pupiled eyes.

■ ■ ■

There are few things in the world that can have the last word as well as a nice blast of pepper spray. Talon, who was the recipient of the angry, acidic burst, had not known that such excruciating pain could exist—and if there had been any doubt in his mind about what an evil place the Topside was, those doubts were now gone. A moment before, he had been trying to calm the screaming girl; now *he* was the one screaming, his eyes, mouth, and nose filled with this spray of flame. The pain went so deep, he felt his legs moving involuntarily, sending him in a blind stumbling fit around the room. Finally his legs gave out, and he sprawled in a bruising slam against the hardwood floor—almost as bruising as the slam to the floor the girl had given him. As Talon gripped his face in blind agony, he was certain that he would die at the hands of the Topsiders.

■ ■ ■

It was all a bit embarrassing for Lindsay. Certainly there was that first moment of triumph as she depressed that little aerosol knob—but as she watched him bounce around the room like a pinball going for bonus points, her sense of empathy kicked in. Clearly this person was not right in the head—one need only look at the way he was dressed: sewn shreds of fabric, a vest made of old paper clips or something of that sort. But it wasn't only his clothes. There was some strangeness in his eyes—or what she had seen of his eyes before temporarily blinding them. He wasn't quite... normal. At least not normal in the way that Lindsay had come to understand it.

Now, after bouncing off the TV, the wall, and the bedpost, he lay on his hands and knees coughing and groaning, completely helpless at her feet, and suddenly Lindsay felt a bit foolish standing there, as if she had used a cannon to kill a fly.

Todd burst into the room not a second later, with a few spectators behind him.

"What's going on up here? Who is that? What's he screaming about?"

Lindsay did her best to explain the situation in twenty-five words or less, and Todd, for the first time in his life, complimented her. "Good for you, Lindsay," he said. But somehow a compliment from Todd didn't make her feel any better about this unpleasant state of affairs.

As Todd wedged his foot beneath the wailing boy's ribs, flipping him over onto his back like a turtle, Lindsay began to feel even more sorry for him. She was warned about this in self-defense class. *Never feel sorry for an attacker, because it makes you a victim twice. Remember—sympathy kills.* But in spite of her karate classes and her no-mercy front, she was, after all, the same girl who had been known to liberate Roach Motels as a child. As she watched the disgust and hatred bloom on Todd's face, she was thankful for her own streak of humanity.

"He's a street freak," Todd announced with a dismissive snarl. "Call the cops to haul him away."

A kid behind him pulled out a cell phone, and New York City's finest were paged to the scene.

"Just kill me," moaned the boy. "Just kill me now."

"Ah, shut up," said Todd, who then hurried off to retrieve his bicycle chain—a tempered steel thing that seemed thick enough to lock down the space shuttle. Then he hauled the fallen boy to his feet.

By now the boy's gasps and wails had become groans and grimaces, and his pain had subsided enough for him to struggle as Todd and four others chained him to one of the thick mahogany bedposts at the foot of Lindsay's bed. "That'll hold him until the trash police arrive," Todd said.

Meanwhile, downstairs came the telltale countdown, and a cheer that echoed throughout Manhattan as the clock struck midnight. Todd took a long, angry look at the boy, who now looked like someone about to be burned at the stake. His eyes, red and teary, strained to flutter open. Then Todd suddenly hauled off and belted him across the face, hard enough to make the entire bed frame shake. "That's for making me miss New Year's."

"You didn't have to do that, Todd," Lindsay said. But he ignored her, sauntering off to wash his fist so as not to catch some street-freak disease.

Todd's friends, who had no intention of missing the

singing of "Auld Lang Syne," even though none of them knew the words, deserted back to the party, leaving Lindsay alone to stand guard. Outside, fireworks lit up the city from the Battery to the Cloisters, and with each explosion, her blinded prisoner flinched.

"It's only fireworks," she told him, keeping a good six feet away from him.

He turned in her direction, straining to open his eyes, but still they would only crack into the tiniest of slits. "You people are cruel and crazy and stupid," he said, his voice raspy and worn from all the screaming he had done. "Just like they say."

Lindsay didn't like the sound of that, mainly because she wasn't sure what he meant by "you people," but, having a background that was two parts Irish, one part Greek, and one part Polish, she found all of her ancestry equally offended.

"Y'know you don't have to live like you do....There are places you could go that can...take care of you...."

He stiffened at the suggestion. "How do you know how I live? You don't know anything about me."

"I know that you broke into my house."

"I didn't break in—your wall was open."

Lindsay glanced into the hallway. Todd had gone downstairs to rejoin his friends. She said nothing for a while, waiting to see what her prisoner would do next. As the sound of fireworks faded, he seemed uncomfortable in the silence. "You people have stupid names," he said. "Todd. Lindsay."

"Thanks a lot, I suppose yours is better?"

"My name is Talon," he said with an odd pride in his voice that made Lindsay laugh.

"Yeah, sure, whatever."

Talon bristled at her laughter, and squirmed against his bonds. "My name found me when I was two weeks old," he said. "When a bat clawed at my cheek." He turned his face to show the faint shadow of a scar beneath his right eye. "See?"

Lindsay took a step closer to see it, fiddling with her braid, which now draped across her shoulder. She wondered if her name would mean more to her if there was a reason for it.

On the dresser was a little spray bottle of water Lindsay used to get knots out of her hair. Now she grabbed it and ventured closer to Talon. "This might sting, but only a little."

She sprayed some water into his eyes. He winced and then blinked, the water running down his face like tears.

"One more time." She hit both of his eyes with the water again, and this time when they cleared, they stayed open for the most part, although they were red and veiny from the pepper spray. He sighed with relief—as if he had really thought he would be blind forever. Lindsay wondered how ignorant one had to be not to know about pepper spray—especially a street person, who was probably threatened by it every day.

He studied her with his bloodshot eyes.

"Why do you wear your hair like that?" he asked. "It looks like a gator's tail—you might as well dye it green."

Lindsay opened her mouth to poke fun at his mane of untamed curls, oddly shaven around the ears, but there was something about it that she liked. So instead she glanced toward his feet, where something else caught her attention.

NEAL SHUSTERMAN

"Well, at least I'm not dumb enough to wear a watch on my ankle."

"We wear our watches low," he said as if speaking to a imbecile, "to remind us that time is of low importance."

She looked at the scratched Rolex, and his pant cuffs, which seemed intentionally frayed. She could find many things about him to mock, but she stopped herself because she didn't want to bicker. She wanted answers. "Why have you been spying on me? Why were you after me?"

He regarded her, his face cold and unreadable. "I have no interest in you."

Lindsay found herself far more disappointed than she wanted to be. "Why not?"

"Because my mother still recognizes me."

"I have no clue what you're talking about."

"No," he said coolly, "you wouldn't."

Clearly this long-haired, odd-clothed, unusual-smelling intruder was trying to trick her in some way—using double-speak to confuse her, catch her off guard. It made her wish she could simply go downstairs until the police arrived to cart him off to the Bronx, or wherever it was they dumped weird-looking transients. But she couldn't tear herself away like that. Besides, this conversation was far more engaging than anything going on downstairs.

"There's a piece of paper in my front pocket," Talon said. "That's why I'm here."

Lindsay's curiosity wrestled with caution, and in the end she stepped up to him, reached into his pocket, and pulled out the paper, reading it. "These are all antibiotics..."

"Do you have any?"

"I don't know. Maybe. Are they for you?"

Talon shook his head. "They're for my little sister. She has a fever, and a bad cough that's getting worse."

"Why don't you just go to a hospital?"

"It isn't allowed."

"And this is?"

Then, for the first time since having his eyes back, Talon looked away from her. "No, not really," he said, and then he looked back at her, offering an apologetic grin. "But it seemed like a good idea at the time."

Lindsay forced back her own grin, determined not to let him see it. "What planet are you from, anyway?"

But he didn't seem to get the question. "What are you going to do with me?"

Lindsay shrugged. "That's up to the police."

Outside, the sound of fireworks became fewer and farther between. A police siren echoed somewhere far off. There was no telling whether or not that particular police cruiser was on its way to this particular break-in.

There were several options in front of Lindsay now, and she began to feel the weight of responsibility on her shoulders. The safe thing would be just to wait until the police arrived to cart Talon away, and she'd never have to deal with him again. The various voices of reason in her head told her to do just that, and she was accustomed to listening to those voices.

But the voice of reason was quite often a coward, and she was tired of having her life ruled by fear. Just because he was too proud, or deranged, to take his sister to a free clinic, it didn't mean Lindsay could just turn her back.

"It sounds to me like a bad case of bronchitis—it's going around. Wait here," she said, as if Talon had any choice, and she went off into the bathroom in search of what he needed.

She had no antibiotics of her own, but Todd might. Lindsay suspected that Todd would never take the full ten days of an antibiotic. Knowing Todd, he'd ditch the prescription the second he was feeling better, and as she opened Todd's medicine chest she found that he was true to form. Inside was quite a little pharmacy of abandoned medications for everything from strep throat to athlete's foot. She knew it was irresponsible, unwise, even illegal, to give Talon what he was asking—but what if the little girl died because Lindsay had refused to pilfer some of Todd's medicine? And so, against a lifetime of better judgment, Lindsay took a half-full vial of Biaxin, which she knew cured a variety of ills, and hurried back to Talon.

Downstairs, the front door had opened, and she thought she heard some voices that wielded a bit more authority than Todd and his friends.

Quickly, she slipped the vial into Talon's hip-pouch. "This is what you need," she told him. "She's little, so break them in half and you'll have enough for ten days—and if she keeps getting worse, you have to swear to me you'll take her to a doctor, whether 'it's allowed' or not."

When Talon reluctantly agreed, she tried to undo Todd's chain. Although Todd was reported to have a decent IQ, he must have cheated on the test, because the chain, although wrapped around Talon and the pole three times, merely had to be lifted high enough to clear the bedpost for Talon to be freed. It didn't take Houdini to do the job.

The instant Talon was free, Lindsay hurried out of the room, for she heard the heavy footfall of the policemen plodding up the stairs. She met them halfway up.

"Officers, thank you for coming," she said, standing in their way as they tried to get upstairs. "It was terrible, he broke into the house—I'm still shaking." Still, she stood in their way.

"Don't worry, miss. We'll take it from here."

They pushed on past her, and Todd led them to her room…where they found the chain on the floor, and no sign of Talon.

"What happened? Where did he go?" yelled Todd. "Lindsay?"

"Beats me," she said. "Didn't you chain him tight enough?"

With nothing else to do, the police took a report, confiscated the spiked punch, and left.

It was as Lindsay was preparing for bed a few hours later that she noticed something on the floor, near the bedpost. A brown sock stretched out and overworn, filled with lines where it had been redarned…but closer inspection revealed that the sock wasn't really brown at all. It was a coarse weave of every color of the spectrum—as if someone had cleaned out the lint-trap of a dryer and woven it into a sock. She had no idea what would have possessed her strange intruder to leave a single sock behind—and God knew how many diseases it carried. But, still, Lindsay kept it, leaving it on her dresser as she began, once and for all, to undo her stiff gator's tail of a braid.

5

Strangers in a Drain

Lindsay knew that in a city of ten million rushing souls, chance meetings rarely happen more than once. Yet she found herself wishing that weren't the case. True, her experience with Talon had been somewhat traumatic—the type of big-city nightmare her mother always warned about. After all, what could be more terrifying than a stranger appearing in her own room? And yet, Lindsay could not get the image of Talon out of her mind. It nagged at her like an itch out of reach.

"I saved Lindsay's life," Todd announced at the breakfast table the following morning. He proceeded to tell their father the complete tale, in a bungee-stretch of exaggeration.

"He was huge," Todd said.

"Not that huge," Lindsay corrected.

"He had these wild, psychotic eyes," Todd said.

"Maybe because I sprayed them with pepper spray," Lindsay reminded him.

"No telling what twisted, demented things he wanted."

"I know what he wanted," Lindsay mumbled.

Needless to say, Mr. Matthias had the fissure between the two upstairs hallways completed immediately, closing out forever that dark space between the walls. For the next few days, Todd was constantly reminding her how very dangerous the situation had been.

"He could have cut you up into a thousand pieces and eaten you one bite at a time," he would say, or, "He could have sautéed your guts in garlic and olive oil." Todd was merciless in illustrating all the ways in which she might have been ingested. Lindsay's personal favorite was: "He could have barbecued your liver and served it up with onions." It made Lindsay laugh because surely no cannibal in his right mind would eat liver and onions.

By the end of her first week of school, she reluctantly had to admit her landing in New York was a crash-and-burn. Her father's schedule left him little opportunity to keep track of Lindsay's tribulations—but he must have sensed something amiss, because he found his way into her room one night as she prepared for bed, and asked the proverbial parental question: "Is everything all right at school?"

Lindsay wondered if there was ever a kid in the history of the world who answered anything but, "Yeah, sure, fine" when the question was posed. "Yeah, sure, fine," she told him.

He sat on the chair beside her as she read a book. Unlike Todd, he didn't use her school supplies to clean his fingernails. "The schoolwork's not too hard? Kids treating you okay?" he asked.

She considered telling him the truth—that Todd had blabbed her New Year's Eve experience throughout the hallowed halls of Icharus Academy so that Lindsay had instantly become known as "that poor girl who was attacked on New Year's Eve" and everyone looked at her as if she would slip into some screeching flashback at any moment.

But what was the point in telling her father that? He would call the school, raise a ruckus, and it would solve nothing, because the problem wasn't the school. It wasn't really Todd, either.

"Things are different here," she told him. "I'll get used to it." But it wasn't just "things" that were different...*she* was different. In any other situation, she would have quickly exerted her own personality and shone through, but the girl who had grown under her mother's tutelage wasn't the girl she wanted to be anymore. The problem was, there was no image rushing in to fill that void. Nothing but the image the Icharus kids tried to pin on her.

"You should have Todd get you an appointment at Hair-On-Fire," her father suggested. "They'll give you one of those nuclear hair creations that will get you into the in-crowd in no time."

Lindsay sighed and put down her book. "Maybe I'll get a few of those chic tattoos, too."

That started her father stammering, like someone who suddenly found himself on the wrong side of a closed window.

"I'm kidding, Dad."

He grinned, dropping his shoulders in relief, then kissed her and left, as if something had been accomplished.

■ ■ ■

With the Icharus crew not worth the trouble, Lindsay found herself alone more often than not during those first few weeks, but she was hardly bored, because she had developed a curious hobby. She spent her free time secretly searching dark, unsafe corners for a trace of the one thing in New York that intrigued her and gave her a hint of mystery: Talon.

Though she tried to avoid it, her search eventually brought her sniffing around the subway, and as anyone can tell you, that is not a pleasant endeavor. The smell of the subway is a unique brew of select garbage fermenting in soot-sifted runoff and various bodily fluids—and when people speak of the special air of life that fills the city, they are probably imagining the smell of the subway. The Downsiders had no love of it—in fact, they had great fans that sent the stench back to the surface, where it belonged.

It was on a bench at the lonely end of the Seventy-seventh Street and Lexington Avenue station that Lindsay found a tattered old woman willing to tell her what she wanted to hear.

"So you've seen one of them!" the woman said, with a voice almost as ragged as her clothes.

"He came to my house. He was looking for medicine."

The woman nodded. "They do that sometimes. So I hear."

"They?" asked Lindsay. "Who are they?"

The woman looked around, as if someone might be lurking in the shadows, listening in. Then she leaned in close to Lindsay. "The Under-Angels," she said. "That's why I wait here. I'm waiting for the day they choose me and take me down to Heaven."

■ ■ ■

Never before had a girl caused Talon so much pain. Perhaps that's why she had left such a lasting impression on him. This Topsider. This "Lindsay."

"Best if you leave it alone," The Champ told Talon over a particularly brutal game of Risk. "You don't break into someone's house and then go asking her out to the movies."

"The what?"

"Never mind," answered The Champ as he proceeded to wipe out Talon's entire Argentinean army. "Anyway, don't they have girls your age down there?"

Talon shrugged. "Yeah...but none of them ever sprayed me with eye-poison."

That made The Champ laugh, and his laughter made Talon angry. He would have to take it out on The Champ's meager forces in England. "Besides, she saved my sister's life...and I have to return her book." He tapped his pocket, where he kept the somewhat dog-eared copy of *The Time Machine* he had salvaged the day he was hit by the brick.

"Those kinds of girls..." said The Champ, "they're not looking for the likes of you."

"So what do they look for?"

"If I knew that, do you think I'd be living at the bottom of a pool?"

Talon looked down at the playing board, studying his

positioning on the landmasses. The Champ, he knew, was one of the Topside's wise ones, but clearly he couldn't answer every Topside mystery.

The Champ had told him that this game board was a copy of the Topside map of the world.

"Where are we?" Talon asked. "I keep forgetting."

The Champ pointed to a spot on the board where orange met blue. "Right here," he said. "East coast of North America."

Talon touched the spot on the map, and then let his eyes drift to the colorful landmasses on other parts of the board.

"And how big is all the rest?"

The Champ raised his eyebrows. "Too big for you to imagine."

Talon nodded and rolled his dice. "Someday, I will be able to imagine all this," he said, "and when I do, she will no longer spray me in the eyes."

■ ■ ■

High up, where inferior concrete had worn away under decades of water erosion, a shaft twisted up from the Downside, to the brownstones of Eighty-fourth Street. For a short time there had been a gateway into the world of the girl named Lindsay Matthias, but now it had been sealed with brick and cement. In spite of The Champ's advice, Talon went there day after day, slipping away whenever he found the chance, to climb into the secret crevice between the two buildings, and listen. The voices came through faint and muffled—even when he put his ear to the cold brick—but enough sifted through for him to know Lindsay's comings and goings. He knew she left at 7:30 every morning and didn't return until 5:30 in the evening, after the sun had freed the sky from its burning rays. He knew that her brother's unpleasant nature wasn't just reserved for Talon. There was a certain melancholy in Lindsay's conversations with her father and brother that made it clear to Talon that she longed to be somewhere else, although he wasn't quite sure where. It brought him a deep sadness to think that she would have to live her life in the Topside—someone with a heart such as hers deserved the dignity of being Down.

These were the thoughts that wove through Talon's mind on the day that he was caught by Railborn.

Lindsay's home was above the untraveled wastes, at the furthest reaches of the High Perimeter—a place of ruined basements and rotting furniture that the Topside had forgotten but the Downside had not yet claimed. Talon thought he was too clever to be followed, but Railborn, as loud and obnoxious as he tended to be, could stalk with the silence of a gopher snake when he wanted to.

When Talon came down from that high crevice, Railborn was waiting for him. With a quick and painful punch to the jaw, he sent Talon sprawling. Talon was quick to react, rising from the floor and butting Railborn in the stomach, knocking him against a brick wall. Furious about this ambush, Talon was merciless in his retaliation, throwing punches long after Railborn had stopped. Finally they separated, listening to each other's jagged breathing in the darkness.

"I thought I could knock some sense into you," growled Railborn. "We're done Catching, so it's time to pull your thick skull down from the Topside and start thinking about

Hunting rotation. We've been waiting long enough—I won't let you ruin it for Gutta and me."

It bothered Talon the way Railborn said "Gutta and me." Lately, Railborn had been doing everything in his power to get Gutta to side with him in all things—as if it were the two of them against Talon. They both knew that Gutta almost always sided with Talon. This time she wasn't, and Railborn was riding it for all it was worth.

"What I do with my free time is my business," answered Talon.

"No, it's not. Because if the others find out you've been surface-peeping, Gutta and I will be septic-deep because we didn't stop you."

"No one will find out," reminded Talon, "if you don't tell them."

"So now you're going to force us to be accomplices?" Railborn struck the wall in anger and stormed off.

Although Talon wished he could just leave it at that, he couldn't. Fistfights aside, Railborn had been a true friend for longer than Talon could remember, so he caught up with him.

"Are you going to tell Gutta?" Talon asked.

"Who do you think made me go after you?"

Talon smiled. "She's worried about me, isn't she?"

Railborn shifted his shoulders uncomfortably. "So what? If I were the one acting like a freak, she'd be worried about me, too."

"Then maybe you should act like a freak more often."

"Ah, shut up."

They made their way through holes and down debris

banks until they reached the well-marked, well-traveled tunnels of home, where the air was warm and the smells and sounds were numbingly familiar. "Why shouldn't I want to know what goes on a hundred feet above my head?"

"Because it's a hundred feet above your head!" answered Railborn. "That place is their curse, not yours."

"And what if they're not cursed?"

"If they're not cursed, then why were they born on the surface? Feel sorry for them if you want, but don't waste your time thinking about them."

There was little sense in arguing this. Railborn spouted Downside doctrine as if it flowed through his veins, and he believed every word of it. Now that his stint at Catching was over, all thoughts of the Topside had drained out of Railborn's mind.

"It's like the sewers, Talon," Railborn said, finally beginning to cool down. "We built the sewers to channel the Topside away from us. You've got to do that with your brain, too."

Talon smiled in spite of himself. "That's what I like about you, Railborn—your mind is like a sewer."

Railborn grinned proudly. "Thanks!" he said.

But if Railborn's mind was like a sewer, then Talon's was a sump, collecting all those things that no one else dared to think about.

■　■　■

At 5:30 the following Friday evening, Lindsay walked home from the library with a high-octane motormouth by the name of Becky Peckerling.

"The kids in class are easy to remember," insisted Becky. "Gary's the one with those designer blue braces; Andrea's the one with stained teeth; Rhonda's are perfect, but that's only because she had them capped; and Reggie has a gap between his two front teeth that he uses to spit water at people." Becky claimed that she wanted to be a doctor someday, but everyone suspected she'd end up a dentist. "Do you think you know everyone now?"

"Yes," lied Lindsay, picking up her pace down Third Avenue. Gridlock had reached a fever pitch, and Lindsay didn't know which was worse: the honking of horns, or Becky's ramblings. Becky was Icharus Academy's one-woman welcome wagon, although few things about her were welcoming. From the very beginning Becky had glommed onto Lindsay like a barnacle to a boat, and Lindsay didn't have the strength to scrape the poor girl off her hull. Everyone else at school kept a carefully measured distance, which was fine with Lindsay. She didn't want to be drawn into a cliquish world of prep-school intrigue—at least not until she knew which clique was worth aligning herself with.

"Lindsay, are you listening to me? Honestly, if you want to know everybody, you've got to pay attention."

Lindsay had already developed the habit of dropping by the library rather than suffering Todd's slings and arrows at home, but the library was no sanctuary because Becky always followed, and her motormouth never ran out of gas.

As they crossed to the south side of Third Avenue, Lindsay's attention was drawn to a rain gutter in the curb across the street. She could swear she saw someone looking out at her. Normally she would chalk it up to her imagination, but recent events made such a sighting much more plausible. She continued across the street, careful not to let on what she had seen.

"Lindsay, do you hear me?" droned Becky. "Hello, Earth to Lindsay."

Now they stood just above the metal ridge where she had seen the pair of lurking eyes. If she was going to make her move, she had to do it now.

"Excuse me, Becky." Lindsay got down on the ground and peeked into the slit in the curb…

…Only to be faced with the surprised eyes of Talon. Ha! She knew it!

"Why are you following me?" she asked, her ear to the asphalt and her face pressing into the rain gutter. "How long have you been watching me? Do you have a problem? Do I have to call the police?"

Caught red-handed, Talon just stammered.

Becky, not catching any of this, cackled her fool barnacle head off, but Lindsay didn't take her eyes off Talon for fear that he might disappear into the shadows again. Talon did try to back away, but couldn't—and for good reason. Whatever else that metallic vest of his was good for, it was excellent for snaring large clumps of long hair—enough hair in this case to make them inseparable. As Talon backed away, Lindsay was pulled into the drain up to her neck.

"Ow!" shouted Lindsay. "Stop it! Stop it now!"

"I can't!"

It was one of those no-win situations. The angrier Lindsay got, the harder Talon tried to pull away, but he only succeeded in pulling Lindsay deeper and deeper into the narrow slit of the drain until she was in up to her waist. With her hips painfully wedged in the ten-inch-wide slit, Lindsay found herself wearing Third Avenue like a tight-fitting skirt.

"Lindsay!" yelled Becky, who obviously had not seen Talon. "What are you doing down there? Come out now! The light's changed!"

But it was no use. All Lindsay could do was kick her legs futilely against the potholed asphalt.

"There's a bus coming!" shouted Becky.

It was the horror in Talon's eyes that made Lindsay panic. In the *Book of Unpleasant Deaths*, being run over by a bus while stuck in a rain gutter ranked right up there with midair collisions and fast-food snipers.

Talon gripped her tightly under her armpits. "This is going to hurt a bit," he said. "I'm sorry." And then he tugged on her three times until her hips finally squeezed through and she fell headfirst into the five-foot-high concrete chamber. A brake squealed, Becky screamed, and when Lindsay looked up, a big black tire rested where her thighs had been a moment before.

Talon let loose a breath of relief.

For an instant Lindsay was furious at him for putting her in this predicament, but then she realized that he had also just saved her life. The feelings of fury and gratitude canceled each other out, leaving Lindsay numb.

They stood there awkwardly in the half-light of the drain, Lindsay's body aching from her curious birth into this place.

NEAL SHUSTERMAN

While Becky continued to scream up above, Talon stepped closer to Lindsay—but only so he could work her hair free from his metallic vest.

"My grandmother made it for me," Talon said. "It's kind of useless, but I've got to wear it, you know?"

Lindsay nodded. "I've got a sweater like that."

Becky was now crouched in the gutter next to the worn wheel of the bus, peering into the drain. Lindsay stepped back so she couldn't be seen.

"Lindsay? Lindsay, are you there?"

Lindsay turned her attention to Talon. "How's your sister?" she asked.

"Better," said Talon. "Your medicine worked."

"I'm glad."

He studied her for a moment. "You look different."

"I lost the gator-tail," she told him. It occurred to her that, had she kept it, her hair never would have gotten caught in his vest, and she never would have been dragged into the storm drain. She wasn't quite sure how to feel about that.

"Lindsay, I can't see you!" whined Becky. "Are you all right down there?"

Lindsay's eyes had become accustomed enough to the dark to catch the glint of Talon's eyes as he watched her. She saw her own curiosity reflected back at her.

Meanwhile, up above, Becky Peckerling found herself caught in a nasty little dilemma: How was she going to convince people that her friend had just dived headfirst into a storm drain? That sort of claim never flew, and people would likely think she was some weirdo. Even now, as she hung her head upside down off the edge of the curb to peer in, she noticed people staring at her strangely. "Lindsay? Are you alive down there?"

She saw only darkness, until Lindsay took a step forward. "I'm all right," she said calmly.

"Thank goodness. I thought you were unconscious, or had a concussion or—"

"Becky, I really think I'd like to be alone for a while, okay?"

Becky opened her mouth, then closed it again, finding herself entirely speechless. Although she had never told Lindsay, Becky's life was filled with a long list of people who did drastic things to escape her company—but this was the first time anyone had climbed down a storm drain to get away from her. "Oh," said Becky. "Are you sure?"

"Positive."

"Well…do you want your book bag?"

"You can keep it for me."

"Okay then…good-bye." Becky rose to her feet, lingered a moment, and then meandered away, not sure whether to feel insulted or impressed by her own ability to move people to extremes.

Becky's departure left Talon and Lindsay very much alone, in spite of the hordes of people marching past just a few inches above their heads—and it struck Lindsay how easy it was to slip into one of the many invisible corners of life.

"Why were you watching me?" she asked again.

Talon reached into his back pocket. "To give you this." He handed her the tattered copy of *The Time Machine*. "I liked it," he said. "I thought it was funny."

"Funny?"

"Yes. The way he made the Morlocks, who lived Downside, the ugly ones, and made all the Topsiders beautiful, when everyone knows it's the other way around. I like this Hugg Wells."

"It's H. G.," she corrected, "not Hugg."

"Maybe I could meet him someday."

"Not likely—he's dead."

Talon took a step back. "I'm sorry."

Lindsay couldn't help but smile. "Don't worry," she said. "It's not like we were close or anything."

And then she reached into her jacket and pulled out from one of the many compartments a worn sock, which she had laundered more than once before she would dare put it in her pocket.

"You left it," she said, and then realized how odd it would seem to him that she was traveling around with his sock. The fact was, she hadn't dared leave it at home for fear that Todd would discover it while rifling through her things and she'd have to explain it. Lindsay had kept it as a kind of trophy, commemorating her first official traumatic New York experience.

Talon refused to take it back. "No," he said, "I didn't forget it; it was payment for the medicine. It's customary to leave it in the dryer, but there wasn't time."

"You paid me with a sock?"

Talon stiffened a bit. "Hey—do you think socks like that grow on walls? That's a sturdy weave!"

"I'm sorry," said Lindsay. "It's a wonderful sock. Thank you."

And she put it back into her pocket, finding herself oddly pleased that she wouldn't be parting with it.

"Maybe...Maybe I could help you," offered Lindsay. "I could help find you a place to live."

"I already have one."

"No, I mean a *real* place. With carpeted floors, and nice furniture, and windows..."

"Why would I want windows?"

Lindsay sighed. "Listen, forget I asked, okay?"

"Would you like to see where I live?" Talon asked impulsively. "Would you like to see the Downside?"

The question caught Lindsay off guard. It wasn't so much what he'd said, but the way he'd said it—in a potent whisper as if it were dangerous beyond words. And what had he called it? *The Downside?* It certainly sounded like more than just some tiny niche.

"Would you like to show me?"

Talon shrugged as if it didn't matter to him in the least, but they both knew that it did. "If you want to," he said.

Lindsay looked to the narrow slit that led back up to Third Avenue. Up above, the world went about its business. Feet shuffled past, but they already seemed distant to Lindsay. She was in no great hurry to climb back into the tumultuous mobs. Then she turned to look down, into the narrow shaft in the corner of the concrete chamber, where a rusty ladder disappeared into darkness.

Surely there were a million reasons not to go, but those reasons felt less important with each passing second. All her life she had lived in fear that her world would be invaded by dark unknowns. Well, it already had. Her mother was off in the wilds half a world away, leaving her with a workaholic father she barely knew and a Neanderthal "brother" who defined himself by his dislike of others.

Lindsay was scared—not of anything coming in through her window, but of the things that were already inside. She was terrified of being a victim of her own life.

At this moment, it seemed the only way out...was down.

She took Talon's hand, surprised by her own boldness. "Take me there," she said, and as they descended down those rust-mangled rungs, she realized that she didn't care in the least if she ever came back.

6

Topsider Down

Lindsay lost her bearings in seconds, and with it, any sense of control. Still, she found strength in her choice to plummet head-on into this unknown. Even as her sense of helplessness grew, so did her resolve not to turn back. Talon drew her through grunge-ridden passageways void of light and filled with sour, befouled air. Sounds were mutated and magnified as if the tunnels were the chambers of an instrument, resonating all around her. Drips of water sounded like a heavy ball being bounced; skittering pebbles seemed more like a flood of rats; and the walls themselves moaned in oppressive sorrow. Lindsay could only assume their ultimate destination would be even more desolate, and it filled her with deep sadness to think that Talon could find comfort in such a bleak, hopeless existence.

He led her through the darkness with a confidence that

made Lindsay grip his hand tighter. "How can you see?" Lindsay asked.

"I can't," he answered so matter-of-factly that Lindsay took it to be a joke at first...but then she began to wonder if people who lived down below might not have evolved some sort of echolocation, like a dolphin or bat.

"You don't need to see," he continued, "if you can follow the breeze."

He made another sharp turn, and Lindsay reached out to feel the damp wall he had just avoided.

"The feel of the air on the hairs of your arms tells you as much as your eyes can," he told her.

"It doesn't work for me. I'm wearing a jacket."

Talon slowed his pace as he considered this. "Why do you people keep your arms covered so much of the time?"

Lindsay stiffened. It was the second time he had placed her in that questionable group known as "you people." Exactly who did he mean by that?

"The same reason as anybody else," she said. "To keep warm."

"But how can you move in the dark without being able to feel the air?"

"I don't. I just turn on a light."

"But isn't that wasteful?"

Lindsay had no comment, so she just shrugged, and wondered if he could feel that on the hairs of his arm as well. Then, in the silence that followed, it occurred to Lindsay who "you people" must have been. Could it be that Talon meant everyone who lived normal lives in the world above?

"How long have you lived down here?" she asked.

Talon stopped in his tracks at the question. "Are you asking me if I'm a faller?"

She had no clue what he meant but didn't want to let on, so she said nothing.

"I was born Down," he finally said, "and to an important family, too."

"Important to whom?"

"To everyone who knows us, I guess. I even had a great-aunt who was Most-Beloved."

"Most-beloved what?"

"You know," Talon said. "The leader. The chosen leader."

"Oh. Kind of like the mayor."

"Yeah, yeah, that's right," he said, but from his tone of voice, Lindsay knew he didn't know a mayor from a minstrel.

They went down a long flight of stairs to a place where the feel of the breeze changed. Lindsay could hear it whistling beneath a doorway where a sliver of light escaped. Talon took a deep, shuddering breath, as if something was troubling him. He hesitated at the door.

"Why are we stopping?" she asked. In the dim light, she could now see him in gray-on-gray. His pupils were wide and vulnerable. She could feel his apprehension as goose-flesh on the fine hairs of her arm, just as surely as Talon could feel the tunnel drafts.

"We've just crossed through the High Perimeter. Through there is the Downside," Talon said, taking another uneasy breath. "No Topsider has ever entered with their clothes, or with their name."

"I prefer to keep both, thank you." She spoke glibly, trying to mask her own growing unease. Talon didn't speak like a homeless boy who had taken refuge in the tunnels, but like one whose home—whose whole way of life—was every bit as rich and complex as her own. She found herself frightened by the sudden magnitude of the unknown beyond the door.

Talon listened for sounds on the other side, and then he leaned against the heavy metal door, which labored open under his weight.

■ ■ ■

A world, regardless of which one it happens to be, is rather ordinary to the souls who inhabit it. A Topsider could see a spray of a billion stars across the heavens each night, and think nothing of their wonder...or sit on the beach before an ocean stretched out to the razor edge of the horizon and be more concerned with the sand that has gotten between their ham on rye than with the majesty of the seas.

It is human nature to take the most magical of worlds for granted, turning each one into a blank canvas upon which to paint the lives of those who would live there. Only an outsider can see a world's wonders for what they truly are. And so it was with Lindsay as Talon brought her into the Downside.

The moment Lindsay crossed the threshold, she was quick to realize that this place was as different from the "High Perimeter" as her own world was. She had come through the rabbit hole into a realm of beauty.

Before her was an old train station—perhaps from one of the first subways almost one hundred years before. But the station was now far more beautiful than when it had been a part of the surface world, for upon the stones and girders of this old station were painted a magnificent feast of hieroglyphics, a multicolored spectacle of lines and texture, like the walls of an ancient temple. Images within words, words within images, intertwined until the whole place seemed to glow with the captured light of an Impressionist painting. Lindsay was surprised to find that the entire chamber, bright as it seemed, was lit by a single bulb dangling from a long cord above them—and even the cord had writing on it.

"What is this place?" Lindsay said, scarcely able to catch her breath.

"Oh, this?" Talon glanced around as if it were nothing. "This is one of the Rune Chambers."

"Who painted all this?"

"We all have Tagging rotation," Talon said as nonchalantly as a mechanic explaining a car engine. "Sometime between twelve years and sixteen, we spend three months in one of the Rune Chambers. We write our dreams, or things that have happened—or things that we wished would happen. What we think about. What we fear. And when we're done, it's here for all time, for anyone who wants to come and read."

"A library!" Lindsay approached a girder where the words and images grew out of a spiral painted so microscopically fine, they could have been done with a single hair of a paintbrush. She tried to read it, but found only some of the words and letters were English. Some seemed Russian, others Chinese, and some were word-pictures—but taken as a

NEAL SHUSTERMAN

whole, the effect was dazzling. If this was Tagging, then it was the graffiti of the gods.

She turned to Talon. "Where's yours?"

He quickly looked away. "I haven't had Tagging rotation." Then he hopped down to the word-painted tracks of the ancient station, pointing at the mouth of the tunnel. "This way."

The air flowing through the tunnel was warm and tropical, with a clean, earthy smell. It was the same scent Talon had brought to her room on New Year's Eve—and Lindsay now found herself regretting that the tunnel had enough light to see, for now she had no excuse to hold his hand.

So taken was Lindsay with these first glimpses of the Downside that she never noticed how uneasy Talon had gotten. He hadn't planned to bring her to the Downside, not in his wildest dreams—well, maybe in his *wildest* dreams—but now that she was here, Talon was septic-deep. This sort of thing simply didn't happen. Aside from the fallers, no Topsider had ever set foot on Downside soil. Of course, there were legends of Topsiders infiltrating many years ago. Such legends always ended with beheadings and other equally bloody business—but then, just about every old legend left someone without a major body part. These were modern times, Talon told himself, and besides, there was no one in power who could order a beheading. Such punishment could only be doled out by the Most-Beloved.

Still, the Wise Advisors—and even worse, his parents— would not be pleased if they found out. Today, however, was market day, which meant that most people were in the Floodgate Concourse buying and selling food and wares. If

Talon was discreet, he could give Lindsay a whirlwind tour and no one would be the wiser.

Lindsay, still oblivious to Talon's concerns, followed him, awestruck by everything she saw. The Rune Chambers and their tunnels gave way to the low ceilings of what Talon called "The Hudward Growing Caverns," places of dim light where mushrooms, lichen, and the like were farmed.

"This is a parking garage!" exclaimed Lindsay.

Talon explained how Topsiders had a tendency to tear down buildings but forget to pull out the roots, sealing them out of sight and memory.

"But aren't you worried that someone will find it?" Lindsay asked.

"A place must be untouched by Topsiders for a dozen years to be considered part of the High Perimeter, and a dozen more to be claimed as Downside territory," explained Talon.

Lindsay listened to his explanation, amazed at how easily a hidden world could grow in the forgotten places of another.

Talon led her through an assortment of remarkable places, each more breathtaking than the last. They passed through the Hot Springs, where an underground river flowed across a series of steam pipes, heating the water that spilled from pool to pool in a series of waterfalls. They crossed through the Brass Junction, a high-domed chamber at the crossroads of two tunnels. It was like a great domed cathedral, and she wondered how such a dome of brass could be forged...until she examined the wall and discovered that the entire Brass Junction was inlaid with outdated subway tokens—thousands of them lining the walls and ceiling.

"This is a very special place," Talon explained. "People are married here, fallers are named here…"

"Fallers?" asked Lindsay.

Talon hesitated for a moment, then said, "Come on, I'll show you."

Lindsay followed him, feeling more light-headed and giddy by the moment. Everything around her was bursting with a magic she had never found in the Surface World. It had to do with the care that went into every inch of the Downside. Every chamber and niche was a work of art, from the corridor walls papered with colorful images from old billboards, to the floors paved with broken fragments of Topside junk. These people had taken the waste of the World and transformed it into something priceless, with all the skill of Rumpelstiltskin weaving straw into gold.

But nowhere was this more evident than in the Grotto of Light.

They wound through a narrow connecting corridor that opened up into a dazzling cavern lit from above and filled with a veritable forest of tropical plants.

"The Downside has several Grottoes of Light," explained Talon. "Some for growing the green crops, and others, like this one, just for fun." He pointed up to the cavern's high ceiling, from which dangled countless crystals and bits of shiny metal, like a giant chandelier. The light from just a few high-wattage bulbs sifted through them, painting shimmering patterns of refraction across the tropical plants and trees—enough to keep them alive and green.

Lindsay could only gape, and Talon smiled. "I knew you'd like this place."

But it was more than just the grand spectacle of this oasis that stupefied Lindsay—it was the shape and structure of the "grotto."

"Why…this is a theater!" she said, and the more she looked around, the more certain she was. Although the seats were gone, the form was unmistakable. Up above were the balcony and boxes, which were also filled with green leafy plants that stretched toward the ceiling. The floor beneath her sloped down toward what was once an expansive stage but was now covered with a thick layer of shimmering sand—a sort of beach, which, Talon told her, was made from pulverized glass bottles.

"But…but what's a theater doing down here?" she asked.

Talon looked at her as if the question made no sense. "Why shouldn't it be here?" he said, leaving her question unanswered.

"There," said Talon, pointing to a scaffold in the corner. "That's one of my fallers."

Atop the scaffold, a man no older than twenty was whistling happily to himself and hanging crystals from the ceiling as if he were decorating a Christmas tree.

"His name was Dunderhead, or Blunderson, something like that. Anyway, the Topside was killing him, so we took him in and made him one of us. A month ago, he almost threw himself in front of a train, and now look at him! I hear he's redesigning the pattern of ceiling-crystals here to create different patterns of colored light."

"Catching fallers…" Lindsay smiled, finally understanding. "We have places up top that try to 'catch fallers,' but they don't always work."

"There's an old Downside saying," said Talon. "'You can't catch that which you stand above.'"

Somewhere up above, a subway train rolled by, its rumble echoing faintly in the tropical theater. The dangling crystals tinkled like a wind chime in a breeze, and several of them rained down into the plants around them.

"Gunderson—that was his name," said Talon. "Problem is, I'm the one who's supposed to give him a new Downside name, but I can't come up with one."

The faller formerly known as Gunderson took a proud look at his redesigned ceiling, then descended to retrieve the few pieces that had fallen.

"I know what you can name him," Lindsay suggested with a grin as she admired the crystalline ceiling. "How about Michelangelo?"

Talon looked at her, not quite understanding. "You mean the turtle?"

Lindsay laughed, wondering how, out of all the aeons of Topside culture, *that* particular treasure had found its way here. "No," she said, "I mean the artist. He painted a famous ceiling."

"Oh," said Talon. "Well, in that case, it's perfect. Michelangelo it is." Then Talon reached down and picked up one of the fallen crystals. "We're always having to rehang these," he said. "It's a real pain." He handed it to Lindsay. "Here—so you'll remember this place."

Only now, at close range, did Lindsay see what these dangling crystals were. "Is that an earring?"

Talon nodded. "They come washing down the Topside drains by the dozen," he said. This one had a ruby surrounded by a cluster of tiny diamonds.

Lindsay held the earring, which seemed even larger in her hand. "I can't take this!"

"Why not? No one will miss it—and it's one less to clean up."

It didn't take much convincing. Lindsay quickly slipped it into her pocket, fending off the feeling that she was doing something dreadfully wrong.

"Thank you," she said, and Talon led her out before the faller soon to be known as Michelangelo could see them.

As they left the Grotto of Light, the whisper of distant voices wafted through the corridor in which they traveled. Lindsay, of course, was not bothered by this, but Talon knew it meant that the market was winding down. Soon, the walkways would be full of people returning home with food, clothing, batteries, and other goods that they had traded for in the many booths of the marketplace. He picked up his pace and began to plot the quickest course to get Lindsay back to the surface.

Lindsay, however, was in no hurry. As far as she was concerned, she could have spent days navigating the Downside labyrinth, like a modern-day Cortez; a great explorer discovering unknown frontiers.

As she tried to turn down what appeared to be just any other empty corridor, Talon tugged her back, spinning her around and toward him like a step from a tango.

NEAL SHUSTERMAN

"We can't go that way," he told her. There was enough light around them for her to see a staircase descending just a dozen yards down the corridor.

"Why not?"

"Because there are some places not even Downsiders are allowed to go."

There was a harshness to his voice that made it clear there was no arguing this point. She held up her hand, feeling a steady heat pulsing out of the corridor.

"What's down there?"

At first Talon didn't answer, but then his face softened just a bit, and he finally said, "It's called the Place of First Runes. It's guarded by fire and two sentry-assassins. Only a Most-Beloved is allowed to pass. The sentries kill anyone else who tries."

She could sense Talon's growing discomfort as strongly as she could feel the heat rising from the Place of First Runes, and she began to wonder exactly what First Runes meant.

"Talon," she asked quietly, "exactly how long has the Downside been here?"

Again, he looked at her as if her question made no sense. "It's always been here," he answered, as if it were obvious. Then, before Lindsay could press him further, he pulled her away. "C'mon—we can't stay here."

Talon hurried her down a different corridor, a wider one lit by stove burners converted into gas lamps that grew from the wall.

In a moment they heard voices, and a shadow approached down the winding corridor.

Although Lindsay sensed no danger, Talon was anxious

enough for the both of them, and the sight of someone approaching brought him close to panic. How could he have been so reckless as to bring her here? What was he thinking? He doubled back with her only to hear the approach of another cluster of Downsiders from the other direction. Frantically Talon scanned the area for options, of which there were few. He remembered seeing a rusted ladder and a closed floor-hatch some twenty paces back. Although Lindsay imagined he knew every nook and cranny of the Downside, it was far from true. The Downside was too large and convoluted to truly know in a single lifetime, much less fourteen years. Talon had no idea where that ladder descended—and what made it worse was the fact that the hatch was sealed. The Downside didn't much believe in closed doors. If an entryway was closed, there was generally a good reason for it. But, Talon figured, any door in a deluge, so he pulled Lindsay down the corridor, hoping to reach that hatch before they were spotted.

The latch on the hatch gave way with a hollow scrape when he kicked at it, and he pulled up the creaky metal door just as figures came into view up ahead. They were traveling without flashlights, but there was enough light pouring in from adjacent chambers that faces could be seen. Faces and clothes. There would be no mistaking that Lindsay was a Topsider when they saw her clothes.

"Hurry." Talon hid her from view, and she descended without complaint, finally accepting the severity of the situation. He would have followed had there been time, but instead dropped the hatch closed as soon as she was out of view, which, he knew, might elicit another spray in the eyes from her when he let her back out again. But moments later he heard a crashing and clattering from beyond the closed hatch—and a yelp of surprise that was quickly silenced. Talon's dread spiked to an unexplored high.

"Talon!" said a booming voice. "Is that you?"

The voice belonged to Railborn's good-humored, if somewhat bombastic, father—an oversized bear of a man, with the unlikely name of Mosquito, which he had shortened to Skeet.

Skeet slapped a heavy hand on Talon's back, as was his habit; and as was Talon's habit, he pretended the slap didn't hurt like hell. "What are you doing here?"

"Just stalling around," Talon answered.

Skeet looked at the other two men with him, and then turned back to Talon with a hesitant pause that made Talon sick to his stomach. He knew what Skeet was about to say.

"Didn't your new rotation start today? Aren't you supposed to be learning the skills of the Hunt with Railborn and Gutta?"

"I...uh, had an errand to run for the hunts master," he said.

A hunter by trade, Skeet was quick to accept the explanation, for he more than anyone would know how the hunts master loved to run the kids in his charge ragged every moment of their rotation. He laughed and said, "In a few weeks I'll be the one running you ragged when I teach you to gut and skin."

Talon hid his grimace beneath a close-lipped grin. Another painful slap on the back, and Skeet and his cronies were gone. The second the coast was clear, Talon heaved open the hatch and climbed down to find out what nasty fate had befallen Lindsay. It was about three rungs down that he found out the hard way what Lindsay already knew: The ladder had broken. His foot fell upon air, his hands slipped, and he plummeted down the shaft into chilly, muck-filled water. He only needed one guess to know exactly where they were now.

Lindsay stood aside, knee-deep in the pitch-black mire, terrified but trying her best not to show it. She had fallen here a few moments before, along with the lower portion of the ladder, which had snapped under her weight. Her only consolation was having the chance to watch Talon do his ungraceful plunge into the water as well—or at least hear him fall, since the place was as lightless as could be.

"If I knew the tour included the sewers," she told him, "I would have worn boots."

"This isn't just any sewer," Talon said, shaking the slime from his vest. "It's the Bot, and we shouldn't be here."

7

The Bot

The Bot was one of the many unquestioned realities of Downside life. It was there, had always been there, and needed no further explanation as far as Downsiders were concerned. Simply put, the Bot was a Big Old Tunnel—a stone-lined cylinder that ran the length of the Downside and beyond. Although its bilgy waters were nowhere near as befouled as the main line, its cavernous twenty-foot diameter made it a sewer to be reckoned with, and it was the last place Talon would have wanted to bring Lindsay.

"I can't see a thing!" complained Lindsay. "Why don't you people carry flashlights?"

"I don't need one!"

As Talon tried to catch a feel for the direction of the breeze, he had to admit how useful a flashlight would have been. But to Downside men, flashlights were considered a feminine accessory, so Talon was left with nothing but his wits, which right now were about as helpful as a match in a gas main. He silently stewed in the cold, wet tunnel, wondering what moron decided that stumbling in the dark was a "guy thing."

"Serves me right," mumbled Talon. "I never should have taken you to the Downside."

"Oh, stop feeling sorry for yourself, and let's just find a way out." Even though their hands were unpleasantly slimy, they kept a firm grip on each other as they moved down the tunnel, groping for another ladder.

Talon heard a scraping sound, and stopped short, listening.

"What's wrong?"

"Shh!" Talon turned his head to get a fix on the sound—its direction, and more importantly, its distance. He waited a moment more, then heard it again. He placed it about five yards away, but it was a much smaller sound than he had first thought.

"It's nothing," he informed Lindsay. "Probably just a throg."

"A what?"

"You know—a throg. They're like big water rats with long, thick necks to keep their heads above water—don't you have them on the Topside?"

"No." She pulled a bit closer to him. "And anyway, rats don't bother me."

"It's not them I'm worried about," he told her.

Being the widest and deepest of the Topside sewer tunnels, the Bot had quite a well-established ecosystem, and rodents were only a small part of the food chain. Talon remembered stories of the Bot from when he was a boy—it was a place of mystery, for it was the one tunnel whose farthest reaches had never been properly charted. It extended into a dark frontier of tributaries, and caverns that were known only as the Beyonds. More than anything else, the Bot had fine disciplinary appeal among parents, as in, "If you don't behave yourself, your father and I will send you to the Bot"; or, "The Bot's full of little boys who hit their sisters"—threats Talon had heard more than once. Of course no one ever threw small children into the Bot, but the mere suggestion worked like a charm. It wasn't only kids who feared the Bot, however. Even among adults, the place evoked a sense of awe, and a reminder that there were forces at work in the universe beyond the work of human, or Topsider, hands, because unlike any other tunnel, the Bot's only connections to the Topside sewer system seemed random and accidental—as if its existence had little to do with anything either world had planned.

"You're afraid of this place," said Lindsay, far more attuned to Talon's emotions than he wanted her to be. "Why?"

He didn't deny the charge. "Some places aren't as friendly as others. There must be things about the Topside that you're afraid of, aren't there? The moon, and all the pinpricks in the night sky—don't they frighten you?"

"They're not pinpricks," answered Lindsay. "They're stars, and they're comforting, not frightening."

Talon tried to imagine how an unreachable expanse above one's head could be comforting, but couldn't. A ceiling that he could reach up and touch with his fingertips—*that* was comforting. Or the distant rumble of the subway up above. Or the dark.

"I think there's some light up ahead," said Lindsay.

And there was—faint, but it was there, a few hundred yards down the tunnel. Talon breathed out his relief. This was one time when light was, indeed, more comforting than the dark.

They picked up their pace as they sloshed their way toward it. "If I were you," suggested Talon, "I would take a bath when I got home." Then he added, "I could give you some soap, if you like."

"That's okay. I think I can find some."

Just then, Talon heard something again, and he had Lindsay stand still once more as he listened. This time it was a much deeper tone, echoing from much further away—something far batward, but drawing closer. Through the soles of his boots, he felt a vibration rising through his legs until it reached the pit of his stomach.

"Oh, no…" He put his ear to the wet wall and could hear it like the approach of a train. But this was no train—and now he could feel the breeze he could not find before, as if air was being pushed toward them from behind.

"What is it? What's wrong?"

Talon turned to look behind them, seeing nothing in the darkness. But he didn't need to see them. He knew.

Talon squeezed Lindsay's hand tighter, so it could not slip out of his grasp. "Run!" he said. "Run and, whatever you do, don't look back!"

■ ■ ■

Lindsay didn't bother to ask for an explanation. Nor did she need to see Talon's face in the shadows. She knew instantly by his tone of voice that this was not about being caught

NEAL SHUSTERMAN

breaking the rules; it was about living, or dying.

She could feel the rumble now, and heard the violent churning of water behind them. At first she thought it might be some sort of flood—a sewer discharge pounding their way—until she heard the ghastly moaning, deep and guttural, of something, no, of a great *many* things, that were very much alive, and bearing down on her and Talon far faster than they could run. She had heard the stories of alligators in the sewers. Now she knew that those tales must have been true, although she never imagined alligators would make that kind of noise.

"There's the ladder," Talon shouted. It was only thirty yards away now, stretching down from a shaft much wider than the one they had first fallen through. "We can make it."

But Lindsay wasn't so sure, for the rumbling and churning was deafening now, and so was that gruesome groaning that reverberated hollowly around them—a sound so strange, and yet oddly familiar.

The light from the shaft ahead lit the way now, reflecting off the slick limestone bricks that lined the Bot, making it brutally clear how far away they still were from the ladder— and although Talon had warned her not to look, she did not want to die without knowing the nature of her end. She forced a glance behind her, expecting to see a pack of toothy, reptilian monstrosities bearing down on them—but that couldn't be further from the truth.

I must be going crazy, she thought. *Those can't be what I think they are.* But indeed they were, and now they were twenty yards and closing....

■ ■ ■

While alligators once had been a legitimate reason to avoid the Bot, sadly, they no longer played a significant part in Downside life. Their meat, once a staple of Downside existence, hadn't been seen on a dinner table for more than ten years.

It was no mystery how the reptiles had originally gotten there—in the good old days, Topside children would buy baby gators on their Florida vacations. Then after an ungrateful nip or an unpleasant tussle with kitty, the baby gators were sent on a one-way flush down into the sewer. Once there, they would begin a new life, and provide many a hero's scar among the proud hunters of the Downside.... But that was long ago. Thanks to those same proud hunters, and the fact that children now returned from Florida with mouse-ears instead of reptiles, the sewer gators had become extinct.

This threw the whole subterranean ecology into disarray, for without an alligator population to thin out their numbers, other creatures began to thrive. And so, in recent years the prevailing nuisance in the sewers of New York City was violent and unpredictable stampedes of cattle.

The bovine menace was first introduced to the Downside by the unexpected incompetence of two Topsiders—Sidney Black and Henry Pitt, who headed the better-forgotten film company BlackPitt Productions. In the mid 1970s, Sid and Henry had shipped in the steer for their subterranean horror epic, *Bull!*, which the producers proudly billed as "*Jaws*, with a cow."

The star bull, as well as his many understudies and stunt doubles, turned out to be lousy actors, and escaped on the third day of filming, disappearing into the depths. In the end, *Bull!* was never completed, BlackPitt Productions went bankrupt, and moviegoers were spared the cinematic spectacle of man-eating holsteins. As fate would have it, however, several of those wayward bulls turned out not to be bulls after all, and, well, nature found its way. The result was several healthy, if somewhat light-sensitive, herds of cattle.

It was a godsend for the Downside hunters. Subterranean life turned the cattle primitively fierce as they stampeded endlessly through the muck of urban waste in search of moss to graze on. At last there was dangerous game once more, and the hunt reemerged as a favorite rotation among the Downside teenagers. Few events were more exciting than the prospect of running with the bulls.

Of course, few people *actually* ran with the bulls. After all, being trampled to death in the sewer wasn't exactly a hero's death—and besides, hunting methods had become more sophisticated than in the days people wrestled alligators by hand. No, only an imbecile on an unlucky day would find himself caught in a down-steer stampede.

■ ■ ■

Twenty yards and closing.

Talon pushed Lindsay in front of him as they ran for the ladder, putting himself between her and the herd, determined that if someone had to be gored by a horn, it would be him. The first of the beasts overtook them, churning past them as if they weren't even there, their maniacal mooing resonating through the tunnel.

In an instant the animals were barreling past them two

and three abreast and disappearing again into the darkness ahead, completely oblivious of the two humans caught in their bone-crushing path. Talon and Lindsay were almost carried away, then Talon reached out and grabbed the ladder. Using all his strength, he pulled Lindsay away from the blind beast that was about to crush her beneath its hoofs. But they were not home free yet, for now the largest of all—an Angus as dark as the pitch it was coming through—was heading directly toward them. There was no question that its head was much stronger than the worn iron of the ladder, and there was no time to climb out of range. Talon and Lindsay could only stare as it plowed toward them.

It would have killed them had salvation not come in the form of a heavy steel disk dropping from the shaft above.

The falling manhole cover hit the bull's shoulder with a *clang,* and with such force that it was knocked out of stride. It stumbled into water, causing a multicow pileup that managed to slow the stampede long enough for Talon and Lindsay to climb up and out of the down-steers' killing path. When Talon looked up, he saw what he knew he would see—because manhole covers did not fall indiscriminately in the Downside.

There, just out of view, toward the top of the shaft, were two familiar kids anxiously chattering with one another, perched like spiders in a web, and wielding a second manhole cover. The hunt had begun.

■ ■ ■

The spiders were Railborn and Gutta, who were tethered from ropes dangling down the shaft, in the midst of their first Hunt. Railborn balanced the second manhole cover, gritting his teeth against the weight, with high hopes of nailing a healthy steer so he could come back victorious on the first day. "Did we get one?" he asked.

"I don't know, I didn't see," said Gutta, peering into the shadows. There had been a momentary slowdown, but the steer all seemed to be plowing past again. If their first shot had hit something, it had only been momentarily stunned. But there was something else down there now. Something moving toward them.

"Wait," said Gutta, "I think there are people down there!"

"What?"

Out of the depths climbed a fugitive of the stampede—a wet, grimy girl. But she wasn't alone. Talon was right behind her.

The shock was enough to make Railborn lose the manhole cover. It went spinning end over end, slamming into the water between cows.

"Great," said Gutta. "That was our only ammo."

"Talon, what are you doing down there?" demanded Railborn.

"And who is this?" asked Gutta angrily. "What's this all about?"

"She's a faller," Talon quickly told them. "She got trapped in the Bot, and I had to get her out. That's all. No big deal."

"Hi," the girl said, and said nothing more.

Gutta scrutinized this "faller," shining her flashlight in the girl's squinting eyes. "If she's a faller, how come I don't remember catching her?"

"I didn't say she was one of *our* fallers. She's somebody

else's—from one of the other groups in our last rotation."

"You were supposed to be here with us!" shouted Railborn. "The hunts-master is blaming us because you weren't here!"

"Well, I'm here now, aren't I?"

Down below, the last of the stampede had gone past. They could hear the distant *clangs* of falling disks as others in shafts further down the hunting route discharged their ammunition.

For Railborn, Talon's actions might as well have been deliberate sabotage. "My father expected me to bring home a kill on the first day," he barked. "What am I going to tell him now?" But Railborn was kidding no one. Even he knew that the real source of his anger was the fact that Talon, once again, had beaten him to the punch. It was obvious to Railborn that Talon had gone down into the Bot as a show of bravado on the first day of their hunting rotation. It was this kind of one-upmanship that always drove Railborn crazy. Tonight Talon would be able to go home and tell his parents and all their friends that he had actually run with the bulls. But what would Railborn have to tell? And although Gutta didn't seem too impressed right now, Railborn knew she would be once she cooled down. Even now it seemed Gutta had completely forgotten that Railborn existed, throwing all of her attention on Talon, and this faller-girl, who, even under the layers of Bot scum, was clearly quite pretty.

"What is that she's wearing?" demanded Gutta. "Are those Topsider clothes?"

"No…," said Talon. In truth, the clothes the girl wore were so covered with grunge, you couldn't tell what kind they were. "Can't we talk about this somewhere else?" asked Talon.

And so the four of them climbed out of the shaft—but no sooner were they out than Talon was slipping away without explanation, taking the faller-girl with him.

Gutta tried to follow, but got caught in her tether and by the time she untied herself they had disappeared down any one of a half dozen passageways. She grunted out her frustration and kicked the wall.

Railborn took a step closer to her, but decided he was too close and backed away again. This may have been the wrong time to say what he was about to say, but it seemed to him this was as close to a right time as he would ever get. "It's okay," he offered, trying to find in his voice the casualness that came so naturally to Talon. "If he doesn't want to be with us, then we can do the rest of the rotations without him. Just you and me."

Gutta didn't say anything. She just looked down the various intersecting passageways around them, still searching for a sign of Talon.

"I mean," continued Railborn, clearing his throat, "there's no law that says he has to be a part of our group, is there? And it would be kind of nice if it was just the two of us. I'd like it, anyway…wouldn't you?"

Finally Gutta turned to him. "What's his problem anyway? He's never around when he's supposed to be—he's hanging out with fallers instead of his friends…" and then she stopped, finally catching Railborn's pleading eyes. "Huh? Did you say something, Railborn?"

Railborn turned his gaze to the dusty stone floor. "Naah," he said. "Never mind, it wasn't important anyway."

Missing Persons

Talon led Lindsay through the darkness of the High Perimeter once more, but this time they moved more swiftly, for Lindsay had grown accustomed to the dark. They emerged through a narrow grate into the comfortable, if somewhat unconventional, "apartment" of an old man Talon called The Champ. Although The Champ had been snoozing in front of his discolored TV screen, he showed his finest hospitality to his guests, offering them each a shower in the pool's old locker rooms, which he referred to as his "bathroom suites." It was a far better idea, thought Lindsay, than stepping out into the cold night with wet, grime-covered clothes.

As Talon's day started at sunset, this was probably still morning for him—but for Lindsay the exhaustion of the night was hitting hard and heavy. It must have been late. She wondered if her father would be home yet, and if he would notice that she was gone.

She stepped out of the girls' locker room wearing the oversized jeans and a flannel shirt that the old man had supplied. He busied himself preparing a skillet of rich-smelling stew over an electric range toward the shallow end of the pool, and when he saw Lindsay he dished her out a bowlful. Until she saw it, she didn't realize how hungry she was, and she shoveled it in as if she hadn't eaten in weeks.

"So you're the girl he's been doin' all the thinking about?" said The Champ, glancing back to make sure Talon was still in the other locker room.

"I suppose so," said Lindsay, not sure whether to be flattered, amused, or irritated by the fact that this was common knowledge.

The Champ grinned. "And I'll bet he was a total gentleman, wasn't he? They're all like that, you know—they got this weird code of chivalry or something. He's not even allowed to look at a girl the wrong way."

"Because his mother still knows him?" Lindsay said, fishing for a clue.

The Champ chuckled. "He told you about that, huh? From what I can figure, the boys down there aren't allowed to date until their mothers don't recognize them anymore—whatever that means."

Lindsay's eyes widened in new understanding, and her lips pursed in secret disappointment. She took a good look at The Champ; his dark, weatherworn skin, his mannerisms, the way he moved. Like someone born to a world of light. "You're not a Downsider, are you?" she asked.

The Champ shook his head. "I'm what you might call an independent."

Lindsay heard the shower turn off in the boys' locker room. She took a step closer to The Champ. "Who are they...these 'Downsiders'?" she asked quietly. "How did they get down there?"

The Champ looked away, returning to his stew on the range. "Who does *he* say they are?"

Lindsay knew what Talon believed—that the Downsiders were always there, before there was a city, before there was even a Topside. But Lindsay had enough perspective on the world to know that it couldn't be true, and as she studied The Champ's face she could tell that he didn't believe it, either.

"You know something, don't you?"

He threw her an uncertain glance. "I don't *know* anything. Not for sure anyway. And maybe some things are best left that way."

"But couldn't you tell me what you think?"

The Champ spooned himself out a bowl of stew and took a long time before answering. "Did you ever hear of a man named Alfred Beach?"

Lindsay shook her head.

"No, I didn't think you would have—he was mostly forgotten by the time I was born."

Talon came out of the locker room then, having redressed in his Downsider clothes, which he had washed and rung out but were still sopping wet. The Champ quickly cut short his conversation with Lindsay. "Like I said, some things are best left unknown."

Talon hopped down into the pool shell. "I was hoping

you could help get her back home," he said. "I would, but I'm in deep trouble as is."

"I'm not exactly an invalid," said Lindsay. "Getting home's a no-brainer. I don't need help."

The Champ laughed. "At two in the morning everyone needs help getting home."

Lindsay gasped. "No! Is it really that late?"

"I guess we're both in trouble," said Talon.

The Champ took a metal tin down from a cluttered shelf and pulled out a few crumbled bills. "I'll give you cab fare and hail you a taxi."

"You'll *loan* me cab fare," corrected Lindsay.

Talon now stood next to the pool drain, looking like a wet puppy, far less threatening than he had appeared to her on New Year's Eve.

"Thanks for showing me all that…," she said, feeling a gap fall between them like the distance between worlds.

"Maybe we could meet here at The Champ's place sometime," he said. "Play a game of Monopoly or something."

"Sure, maybe," said Lindsay.

"You can even be the car," said Talon. He lingered a moment more, then slipped down the drain and disappeared. Lindsay listened until the sound of his footfalls in the tunnel became too distant to hear.

■ ■ ■

In the double town house on Eighty-fourth Street, Mark Matthias had indeed noticed that his daughter wasn't home—and the fact that he hadn't noticed until about 9:30

at night only fueled his fear and frustration. At first he foisted the blame on Todd, who was supposed to be looking out for Lindsay but who hadn't noticed she was missing until his father pointed it out. But as the evening went on, Mr. Matthias took on more and more of the blame himself.

Becky Peckerling, who was the last person to see her, said only that they had parted company at about 5:30 on the corner of Third Avenue and Seventy-seventh. Becky failed to mention, however, that the last place she had seen Lindsay was *under* Third Avenue—which would have put an entirely new spin on the unfolding investigation and would have left Becky the subject of more interrogation than she cared to handle.

"Maybe that street freak from New Year's Eve kidnapped her," suggested Todd. And so the police prepared an all-points bulletin featuring a sketch of Talon that didn't look anything like him. Before the sketch could be released, however, Lindsay showed up on her doorstep wearing clothes that clearly were not hers.

"My God, Lindsay! Are you all right? Did they hurt you? Did you get a good look at them?" With all those hours to dwell upon what fate might have befallen the poor girl, it was already her father's foregone conclusion that she had been the victim of foul play.

Lindsay knew she couldn't tell where she had been and what she had seen. But she was not a liar by nature and, frankly, she was in no state to attempt any explanation at all.

"I'm tired, Daddy, and I really don't want to talk about

it," she said. Then she plodded upstairs to her room, taking some guilty pleasure in the fact that she had left her father and Todd completely stymied. But her father could not leave it at that. In a few minutes he came to her room. Lindsay found herself both frustrated and yet in some small way pleased that he would not let it slide.

"I *am* your father," he said as he stormed around the room. "I think I'm entitled to know where you were until three in the morning."

Lindsay would have feigned amnesia if she'd believed it would fly…but her father was right: He did deserve some sort of explanation, a half-truth at the very least.

"I thought I'd take a tour of the subway," she told him, "but I guess I took a wrong train and ended up lost in a place I'd never seen before. I would have called, but I felt so stupid about the whole thing, I just wanted to get home."

Her father scrutinized her, clearly wrestling with how much of the story he should buy. "And the clothes?"

"Oh, that…well, my clothes sort of got…trampled.…But I met some nice people who gave me clean clothes and cab fare. You know, people here aren't as nasty as everyone says."

Her father paced the room, obsessively rubbing his allergic nose.

"Daddy," she asked, remembering what The Champ had said to her, "did you ever hear of someone named Alfred Beach?"

Her father spun on his heel at the mention of the name—something Lindsay hadn't expected. "What about Alfred Beach?" he asked suspiciously. "Who said anything about *him?*"

Lindsay just shrugged in her own ignorance. "I just heard someone talking, that's all."

Her father hesitated, as if weighing whether or not he should say anything at all. "Alfred Beach was a kind of engineer," he finally told her. "An inventor—a crazy one—who lived a very long time ago."

"Oh," said Lindsay, realizing too late that she had inadvertently tripped a land mine. She could imagine her father, with his grandiose aqueduct dreams, being compared to an old-time crazy by his coworkers. It must have been quite a sore spot with dear old Dad. "Well, I'm sure you're nothing like him," she offered, and began to wonder what a disreputed engineer might have to do with Talon and his world. She wanted to press him further—but then she would have to tell him why she wanted to know, and that was something she had no desire to share. There were so few things she shared with him these days. Since she had arrived they hadn't had a single conversation worth remembering—and it was more her fault than his. His long hours just made it easier to blame him, that's all. The truth is, she hadn't even given him the box of odds and ends that her mother had decided he should have, for fear that the little shoe box of memories might spark some unwanted conversation between her and her father—so she had never even taken it out of her suitcase.

Her father paced a bit more, and finally his eyes zeroed in on hers. "After what happened tonight, I don't want you to go anywhere in this city without your brother anymore."

"He's not my brother."

But her father refused to speak to that. "You heard me," he said, making sure to have the last word as he left.

■ ■ ■

By the time Talon arrived home in his family's private little corner of the world, his clothes had dried enough for his mother not to notice. She sat in their modest but comfortable living area, patiently listening as his sister read from a worn Downside reader.

"How was the first day of the Hunt?" his mother asked.

"Great," said Talon. "The bulls were running. I didn't catch anything, though."

"It's only your first day. Give it time."

Talon quietly slipped into his room and drew the leather room-divider, needing the time alone to sift through the many layers of sediment building up in his brain. He was always a kid who traveled on the fringe of the rules and he could always get away with it, perhaps because he was so well-liked. But bringing a Topsider Down, that was more than bending the rules—it was a cardinal offense, the kind of thing that would shame his family's good name for generations.

But if it was so awful, then why did he find his thoughts so drawn to Lindsay's world? Perhaps because he wanted to be the one to catch Lindsay and rescue her from that sun-blinded Topside life, so full of mysterious temptation—like the taste of snow, or the sight of rushing cars.

He shook his head and laughed as he considered how he might bring the subject up with his father. He was an understanding man, but limited. His life revolved around his trade, and if conversation ever strayed from fishing, he had nothing to say. Talon imagined himself fishing in the main line alongside his father, as he had done for so many years, and trying to breach the subject of the Topside.

"Keep your head in the ground where it belongs," his father would say, shutting him down even before Talon could get to the point. "There's plenty of fish in the pipes," he'd tell Talon; or, "If you don't bite, you can't get hooked."

As the son of one of the Downside's most respected fishermen, Talon was expected to take on the trade after all his rotations were done. Talon never minded the idea, until now. It was an easy path for him—a "no-brainer," as Lindsay would say. But now Talon felt something shifting in himself—something bright and dangerous, realigning his heart toward a new purpose. He wasn't certain where it would lead, but he did know that he would not be his father's son. The prospect thrilled him almost as much as it scared him, and he wondered if the Fates would punish him for being so brash and defiant.

Talon approached the mirror on his wall. *What does this Topside girl see when she looks at me?* he wondered. His face was far from perfect: There was that scar above his right eye; his ears stuck out a bit too much; and then there were his feet, threatening to be even larger than his father's were— useful for balance in slippery places, but still not something to look forward to.

When he turned, he caught his mother spying on him through the divider.

"See anything new in that handsome face?" she asked.

     NEAL SHUSTERMAN

"Sure I do." Talon studied his jaw line, then took notice of how his rounded boyish nose was becoming the strong rigid nose of a man. "Getting so I'll bet you barely recognize me anymore."

"Oh, I think I'll recognize you for quite a while," she said with a smirk, then she left him to grapple with her answer.

Low Justice

A single sentence was engraved on the wall of the Brass Junction:

FEAR THE TOPSIDE, OR BE CRUSHED BY ITS EMBRACE.

It was the single most powerful piece of Downside doctrine; all rules and rituals grew from that belief. Fallers were stripped of all but their soul; the no-man's land of the High Perimeter was established; children were taught the evils of daylight, all to keep the worlds from touching, for it was believed that the slightest brush of one against the other could end both.

As a good citizen, this was something Railborn believed with all his heart. He knew what he was doing when he descended to the low dwellings—the fine apartments where the Wise Advisors lived. He had thought the whole thing through, and although the decision left him with a brutal case of the sweats, he knew he had to notify the Wise Advisors of what he had uncovered since his and Gutta's strange encounter with Talon above the Bot.

"I believe a Topsider has seen the Downside."

He stood in the doorway of the Fourth Advisor—a stocky, gray-haired man who had once been a baker before attaining this position of honor. Railborn chose to tell him rather than any of the other Advisors, because of his mild manner, evenhanded counseling, and his disarming, grandfatherly smile.

But the man's smile faded at the mention of a Topsider. Now he regarded Railborn as if he were the culprit and not just the messenger. "A Topsider? What are you talking about? How do you know this?"

Railborn stammered for a moment, cleared his throat, and stood straighter, determined to get it out. "I know because I saw her myself, Wise Advisor. I've spoken to everyone on the last Catching rotation—no one caught a girl our age, so I know she's not a faller."

"This is serious business. Come, sit down." The Wise Advisor led him into his inner parlor, a spacious and well-adorned room. The low dwellings were larger and quieter than most, because advising wisely required a large, quiet place to ponder weighty questions.

Railborn sat down in a comfortable patchwork chair, and the old man sat across from him. "You've done the right thing coming here."

"I know." Railborn let his eyes wander around the room, decorated with only the best polished hubcaps and plastic knickknacks collected over many years. Gifts for solving disputes, no doubt. With trophies like these, Railborn felt comforted that he was now in the best of hands.

"This Topsider—how did she get here?" the Wise Advisor asked, his hands crossed calmly on his knee.

"She was brought here," Railborn answered evasively.

"By whom?"

"A Downsider."

"*Which* Downsider?"

Railborn had no rope left to dangle on, so he let go, setting the truth in free fall, and putting his faith in the Wise Advisor's ability to fix all things.

"Talon Angler," Railborn said. "Talon Angler brought her here."

The Wise Advisor showed a moment of surprise, but quickly covered it. It was obvious that he knew Talon. But then, everyone knew Talon. Many people knew Railborn, too, but more often than not he was just known as "Talon's friend."

The Wise Advisor pursed his lips. "These are difficult times," he said. "People think they can do as they please, with no consequences to their actions...."

"There's no one to lay down the law," agreed Railborn.

"Well, we need to make an example of Talon so this sort of thing won't happen again," the Advisor decreed. Then he regarded Railborn, eyebrows raised. "What do you think Talon's punishment should be?"

"What do I think?" Railborn looked down. "Well...I think he should be pulled out of Hunting rotation," suggested Railborn—a punishment that, not coincidentally, would leave their little trio a duo. A nice fringe benefit of having done the right thing.

"And?" prompted the Wise Advisor.

"Uh...*and* he should have to make up for what he's done." Railborn imagined three months of slime-scrubbing might humble Talon a bit.

"And?"

"And?" Railborn hadn't considered any more "ands"—but this was why Wise Advisors held their positions: They were the ones who always thought one step beyond. "And," concluded Railborn, "he should be stopped from ever going to the Surface again." He imagined that if Talon were no longer allowed to roam the High Perimeter, he couldn't be tempted by the Topside. *Talon will thank me someday,* thought Railborn. *When he's free from whatever spell that Topside girl has put him under, he'll thank me for saving him.*

The Wise Advisor studied Railborn a moment more, a hint of that warm smile returning to his face. "You're Skeet Skinner's boy, aren't you?"

"Yes," said Railborn, impressed to be recognized, even it had taken all this time.

"Your father keeps hinting that you possess all the qualities of a Most-Beloved. I can see now that he's right."

Railborn beamed. "You really think so?" It was something he never dared to speak aloud, although he dreamed of it often...but to be complimented in this way by a Wise Advisor was more than just a daydream. He couldn't wait to tell Gutta!

The Wise Advisor slapped his knees and stood up. "Very well, then, we'll do exactly as you say: Talon will be pulled from his rotations, made to pay for what he's done, and we'll make certain he never goes to the Surface again."

Railborn said a respectful good-bye and left, bloated with civic pride and a sense that all wrongs would soon be righted, thanks to him, a leader in the making.

■ ■ ■

By the time the Downside rose to greet the new night, a rumor was shooting through the pipes that someone was about to be executed.

Guesses flew as to who the unlucky outlaw might be. Was it Tesla the Tapper, who was known to bribe Wise Advisors with free electricity taps from the city's best transformers? Or maybe it would be Maggot the Tanner, who was once caught trying to pass off leather as fine vinyl.

Railborn knew that they all were wrong, and he raced to catch up with the execution party only to be turned away by a guard at the entrance to the Brooklyn Battery Passage. His heart was now filled with a hopeless sense of doom as he sat there, head in hands, at the passage entrance, and it occurred to him how just a few words spoken to the wrong person could crush one's entire world.

10

Dead Man Flushing

When it comes to world-shattering events, history has a short and selective memory. The great San Francisco earthquake of 1906 lives on in public memory, but no one remembers how, only ninety-six years earlier, a quake hit New Madrid, Missouri, with such force that it made church bells ring in Boston and made the mighty Mississippi River flow backward. Popular memory recalls how Pompeii was buried under the ash of Mount Vesuvius thousands of years ago, but fails to consider the Tunguska Comet blast, less than one hundred years ago, when a stray piece of sky hurtled to earth and leveled a Siberian forest.

Likewise, no one recalls the Great Sinkhole of 1885, when, late in an otherwise uneventful July night, two entire city blocks plunged through one of nature's nasty little trapdoors. It took a two-hundred-foot ladder and a full day to evacuate the hundreds of theatergoers from the ruined

Plymouth Theater, which had resided near the corner of Sixth Avenue and Sixtieth Street.

The event would have been front-page news had not former president Ulysses S. Grant died that very day, thereby diverting everyone's eyes elsewhere. Since all souls were accounted for and there was no loss of life to sensationalize, the Sinkhole of 1885 was treated as small news by the press.

If anyone had thought to probe deeper, however, they would have found that this wasn't so much an Act of God as it was an Accident of Beach—Alfred Ely Beach, to be exact. But, because Beach was the publisher of the *New York Sun*, he had quite a lot of pull in the news media, and succeeded in keeping public attention away from the city's largest pothole.

As luck would have it, the sinkhole was conveniently located right at the southern end of Central Park—and since the building of Grant's Tomb further uptown was a much higher priority, the city decided quietly to build a platform over the whole mess when no one was looking, and extend Central Park one block south. No one argued, the whole affair was quickly put out of mind, and the Plymouth Theater was instantaneously and utterly forgotten. All that remains is the common expression "down in the 'mouth"—although no one remembers the true origin of the phrase.

While the trial and execution of Talon Angler can hardly be considered an earth-shattering event, it does happen to be a key link in the chain of events leading up to the Great Shaft Disaster—a catastrophe that is bound to have staying power in somebody's history book, somewhere.

■ ■ ■

Justice in the Downside was a swift thing, dispensed by the Wise Advisors in small rations. There were no juries, no appeals—it was generally accepted that the Advisors' decisions were always just, even when everyone knew they weren't. Regardless, Downside justice was always quiet—for without the support of a Most-Beloved, it served the Wise Advisors' interests to make ripples of justice rather than waves, lest someone more popular than they rise to defy them.

But who would challenge an act of treason?

Treason. The word hit Talon's ears with the same shock that it hit his parents'. Such a vile, stone wall of a word, for the simple act of sharing his world. But when the Advisors woke him at dusk, dragged him down to their chambers, and asked if he denied the charge, he could not.

They invoked those words engraved on the Brass Junction walls, insisting the Downside must have nothing to do with the Topside—not now, not ever.

"We can't live by that law!" said Talon, rising to his own defense. Everyone—even the Wise Advisors—knew small acts of treason were committed every day…for as much as the Downside's beliefs depended on shunning the Topside, Downside reality depended on *using* it—from secret night raids for batteries and bulbs, to socks left behind on subway vendors' racks as payment for soda and chocolate bars.

"Why was it so wrong to bring her here?"

"Because it's the law!"

"Why does it have to be a law?"

"Because it is."

"That's not good enough!"

He looked around to see if there was anyone who might listen. But there was no one but his anguished parents, and the Advisors. Although all trials were public, the Downsiders rarely attended, because they knew that to look upon someone else's misery was to increase their own. It was a noble philosophy, and one that ensured there would be no resistance to bad decisions.

"Why are you doing this to me?" Talon finally asked before they announced his sentence. They looked away without answering. But Talon knew the answer. It was because anything less would expose the Wise Advisors for what they really were: a weak and useless gathering of fools. At least now they would be a gathering of fools to be reckoned with.

But though they might have been fools, the Advisors knew an easy mark when they saw one. The way the Advisors saw it, Talon was no martyr—he had no cause, no followers. He was just one in a hundred rotation-aged kids, important to nobody but himself, and his family. He would be forgotten—but his crime would be remembered. If this boy's prompt removal could bring a generation to their senses, it was well worth the price. And so they felt no remorse in sentencing him to death.

■ ■ ■

As everyone knew, death's first stop was Brooklyn.

Perhaps that's why Brooklyn was a place feared and respected by the Downside. There was only one Downside tunnel that led there—a straight, solitary stretch that crossed beneath the East River and continued many miles until dead-ending at the Aquatorium, that lonely place where the dearly departed were dispatched to the next world.

Talon was denied the honors of a final meal, or a moment of silent reflection in the Grotto of Last Light. The procession through the Brooklyn Battery Passage, only an hour after his sentencing, was a meager one. There were his parents, who, at Talon's request, did not bring his sister; two Wise Advisors; and three brawny enforcers pulling up the rear, just in case Talon had any thoughts of escaping. In a way it disappointed Talon that his execution was of such small consequence that only two of the five Wise Advisors bothered to come.

A single flashlight lit the way—a dim oval stretching before their feet—but this was one journey Talon would much rather have made in the dark. Unlike the other Down-side tunnels, this passage was narrow and cold, with no doors or junctions. Its air was as stale as death, and every step made it increasingly clear that there was no turning back. The relentless monotony of the tunnel's own walls was a reminder that everyone would eventually make the journey to Brooklyn.

As they silently made their way down the tunnel, Talon tried to find some greater purpose in all of this. He tried to convince himself that perhaps Lindsay was worth dying for…but he didn't know her well enough to know if she was worth dying for. Their friendship was just a curiosity at best, and now it would never be anything more.

How could I be so stupid, Talon thought, *to throw away my life for a taste of snow and the sight of a Topside girl?*

Finally the narrow corridor opened up into the uninviting chamber of the Aquatorium, a jagged cavern where gnarled tree roots wrapped around a ceiling of heavy pipes. At the far end a darkly dressed undertaker waited by a heavy lever.

Talon looked up to see a wide red ceramic pipe dripping with cold condensation and hissing with the rush of millions of gallons of water. This was the Bensonhurst water main—a lifeline that quenched the thirst of the mysterious Topside borough. The Topsiders here never noticed or missed the short surges of water that were regularly rerouted from the water main and into the Downside funeral siphon.

The siphon itself was a narrow rusting pipe, level with the Aquatorium floor. Like so many things in the Downside, it gave the impression that it had been here eternally and had always been meant for this one final purpose.

The Fourth Advisor—the one who had first brought the charge—stood on the platform before the siphon and signaled for Talon to step closer, which he did on unsteady knees.

"You have been sentenced to judgment in the Great Beyond," he said with as much formality as he could muster. Talon heard his parents weeping behind him and cursed the Wise Advisors for forcing them to witness this.

"Do you have any last words? Anything you say will be inscribed in the Rune Chambers."

The suggestion made Talon furious. There were so many

things he had planned to write in the Rune Chambers when his Tagging rotation came, but nothing that could be boiled down into a single set of last words. The only thing he could think to say was, "Tell Railborn he can have my bottle-cap collection."

There was a hole about six feet long in the siphon pipe, and Talon was ordered to climb in. Only now did it finally hit him exactly what his fate would be, and he found his muscles locked solid, unable to move. The enforcers had to carry him. As they did, he frantically began reciting old nursery rhymes in his head, desperate to keep from thinking more than one rhyme into the future—because he knew if he did, he would turn into a screaming, struggling child. For the sake of his parents, he was determined to keep his dignity...but the moment he was laid on his back and he felt the coldness of the pipe seep into his clothes, the fear ripped through him, exiting his mouth in an uncontrollable wail.

"Mom...Dad..." he found himself calling out. *"Mom, Dad, I'm scared...."* He shut his eyes tight, praying that this would all go away and he could just be a simple Downside kid catching carp alongside his father, never thinking of the Topside again. But when he opened his eyes there was no last-minute reprieve—only the somber face of the undertaker, with his hand on the heavy lever.

"May the Fates have mercy on your soul," he said, then pulled back on the lever, sending a mighty surge of frigid water exploding through the pipe, coursing around Talon's body and propelling him feetfirst toward the Land of the Dead.

■ ■ ■

With his world and his life behind him, Talon flushed through darkness, riding the cold surge, gagging, choking, almost drowning in the rushing water. It nearly overtook him, but then he found that if he tilted his neck forward, the water coursing around his head formed a pocket of air and he gulped short breaths every few seconds as he flew on the crest of the wave toward his end.

As he careened through the darkness, he tried desperately to fight the fears that threatened to overwhelm him just as certainly as the water would. What was waiting for him up in the tunnel? Final judgment in the place where all souls go? Or what if there was no Land of the Dead—what if, after all he had been taught to believe, there was nothing up ahead? What if the pipe spat him and all the dead out into an eternal bottomless pit? Or even worse, what if that pit had a bottom?

He was carried for miles, coughing and sputtering, fighting for every measure of breath in the midst of the churning water. *What if it's just this pipe,* he thought; *a straight and endless flow of cold, angry water forever and ever?* But no sooner did he think that than the angle of the pipe changed, heading down a steeper slope, drawing him toward whatever might await him.

He gritted his teeth and pulled his elbows tightly against his body, preparing himself. And when he thought he could not bear a moment more, the pipe was suddenly gone, and gravity took over. Talon yelled as he fell through the void, then his voice was silenced by an icy chill many times colder than the water that had carried him here. It filled his mouth and nose with a bitter, salty taste.

This was death; a wet, lonely hell of frigid salt water. His eyes stung as he tried to open them. His head felt as if it would shatter from the cold. Never before had Talon seen water enough to sink in. The Downside Hot Springs were only four feet deep—but this, this was an abyss. This was the bottomless pit he feared, and it was filled with killing water. He sank, releasing himself to the chill, knowing there was no sense in fighting it now.

Then something snagged his arm. A creature. No—no, a person, pulling him through this liquid eternity, until his head broke the surface and his lungs spewed out the water and drew in a choking gasp of air.

"I got you!" said a woman's voice, raspy and unfamiliar.

Talon could only cough in response. He did not have the strength to resist. He let himself be carried over the waters by this mysterious savior, who could actually float on this vast puddle—not only float, but move, kicking her legs and stretching an arm before her, pulling them both along.

Around them, the waters conspired to take them down, raising and dropping them with a slow, undulating rhythm, curling and crashing over their heads over and over again, until Talon finally felt ground beneath him, and the strange living water pulled back away from them in defeat as they stumbled on soft, sloping earth.

The wind ripped at him now. His muscles cramped into tight, useless knots, and his jaw locked so tight, he could not even shiver.

"Over here," said the woman, dragging him through the coarse sand beneath them. In a moment he felt the pressure of a blanket over his numb body, and another and another—heavy blankets wrapping his body, silencing his thoughts until nothing was left but the will to sleep.

■ ■ ■

Downside, Talon's family received the comforting solace of visitors, their condolences heartfelt, if somewhat trite.

"You'll make it through this," Gutta's mother tearfully told them, with the certainty of a woman who knew grief well, having been made an early widow by a steam-tapping accident. She clasped little Pidge's hands in her own, saying, "Just think of Talon as asleep; resting in peaceful slumber." The woman had no idea how right she was.

After a long, dreamless slumber, Talon opened his eyes to find himself staring at a low, wooden ceiling. He pressed his tongue to the roof of his mouth, tasting a strange bitterness in his throat that wasn't entirely unpleasant.

"You're awake," said a woman's scratchy voice.

He turned his neck to see her, but found that his neck moved like a rusty gear.

"Thought I lost you during the night. Practically had to set you on fire to keep you warm. Here, more coffee?"

She poured a hot, black brew down his throat, and Talon recognized this as the taste he had woken up with. How much of this black fire had this strange woman filled him with? He coughed but swallowed all the same, the warmth of the brew feeling good in his gut.

Slowly, the events that had led him here came back to him. His swift sentencing and immediate execution; the journey to the Land of the Dead—which was not land at all, but water.

This wasn't death, however—he knew that now. Some-thing must have gone wrong—the pipe must have ruptured before reaching its final destination and belched him out somewhere else. A place where the ground was sand, and the ceiling was dark planks, held up by wooden piles.

The woman who attended him had all the semblance of a faller. Her clothes were tattered Topside rags, her hair was a matted red mess, and her lack of teeth made her lips flap around a weakened jaw, turning her speech slippery.

"Lucky I saw you come out of that pipe, yesiree," she said. "Ain't never seen no one sewer-surfing before, and I thought I'd seen just about everything!"

She moved aside, and Talon's eyes were assaulted by a bright light. He squinted, unable to look at it. "What is this place?"

"You're in Coney Island," she said brightly. "Under the boardwalk—like the song."

Still, the light invaded Talon's sensitive eyes. Even when he put his hand before his face, he could see it between the gaps in his fingers.

"That light—can't you turn it off?" he asked.

The woman looked at him for a moment and laughed. "Only the good Lord himself can turn that one off, yesiree."

Talon did not appreciate being the butt of a toothless woman's joke, so, although his muscles felt like old chewing gum, he rose to his feet. "Never mind, I'll do it."

With a blanket wrapped around himself, he stumbled toward the light...

...and in an instant found that the light was no longer just in front of him—it was all around him, turning the sand beneath his feet blinding white. The low ceiling was gone, replaced by shapeless swirls of blue and white—and that light—it was deceptively distant, and infinitely bright. Burning…like the killing rays of the—

The moment he realized what that light was, he fell to the ground, wailing, digging his forehead into the sand, as if he could bore his way back to the Downside.

I'm on the surface…I'm on the surface, and this is daylight!

Instantly the fear, the helplessness that had filled his journey down the pipe came back to him in full force as he lay there, curled up, waiting for the sun to consume him, burning away his brain as it burned away his flesh.

But that didn't happen.

In fact, the burning light actually felt…good.

Still, it seemed an eternity until he summoned up the courage to lift his face from the sand. Slowly he arose, brushing the sand from his face, his eyes adjusting to this new realm of light. Fighting all the Downside warnings that now played in his head, he dared to look at the sun-bleached world around him.

To his right a strand of sand stretched as far as the eye could see, and to his left was a mound of jagged rocks, and the rusty pipe that ejected him here. Up above, pigeons flew freely across an unshielded treacherous blue dome, filled with puffs of white that hung motionless and weightless. But more incredible still was the view directly in front of him. The ball of the sun sat on a shelf—a shimmering blue ledge that seemed built only to hold it. But this was no ordinary ledge. There was a sound calling out to Talon now. It was deep and powerful, yet comforting, like the gentle rumble of a distant subway.

Wishhhhhh, the sound said to him. *Roarrrr…Wishhhh…*

It was the same sound he had heard when the toothless woman had pulled him from the ice-water hell during the night. With the blanket still pulled around him to protect him from the cold, he strode toward that sound, and toward the ledge that held the sun. And that's when his eyes came into sharp enough focus to realize it was not a ledge at all.

If someone had told him of a place like this, he would not have believed it. If someone tried to describe it, he would not have understood. How could he? For before him lay an expanse of deep water that stretched out so far it touched the dome of the sky. So huge was this pond that the water actually rolled in *waves!* It rippled like a deep green sheet toward the end of the universe; it leaped at the sand both angrily and playfully at the same time, shattering and retreating, only to leap again and again. It was so immense, he feared his mind would never wrap around it.

Talon felt faint, and realized that for the longest time he had forgotten to breathe.

"Whatsamatta?" said the woman, coming up behind him. "Ain't ya ever seen the ocean before?"

"No," said Talon, too overwhelmed to offer her anything but the truth. She only laughed and returned to her spot under the boardwalk.

Far out, halfway to the sun, a tiny, tiny vessel floated on the surface of this ocean…but Talon had figured out enough to know that this vessel wasn't tiny at all. It just seemed that way. Maybe it was filled with hundreds of Topsiders, doing Topside things on the Topside ocean, beneath the burning—no—the *warming* rays of the sun.

Talon pulled the blanket tighter as he stood there, the icy water lapping at his feet, and did something he hadn't even done at his own "execution." He cried. He cried for all his Downside years of not knowing miracles such as these. He cried for all the things he suddenly realized he did not know…but most of all he cried for that part of himself that had just been killed forever by his first sight of sea and sky.

11

Surface Tension

Foreigners in any land are usually easy to spot, whether it's an American on the Acropolis, or a Latvian in Laguna. They invariably wear short pants with hiking boots and black socks. They stand uncomfortably close or awkwardly distant when they speak. They dress in ties and skirts that are an inch too narrow, too long, or too short, as if their entire wardrobe is syncopated one beat out of trend. Their faces bear the creases of exotic expressions, and they are forever doomed to appear, in the eyes of the locals, either too sheepishly wide-eyed or too cynically pinched. For all these things they are simultaneously adored and despised by the natives, because they are so elusively different.

But Talon, who had never been anywhere, and didn't know a tourist from a florist, had no training in how to be appropriately foreign. Instead, he flitted along the boardwalk of Coney Island with such hyperkinetic abandon, people merely assumed him mad. Such an impression helped Talon in the long run, because it turned him from being a potential target for crime into a touch-me-not. Surely if there were any hoods strolling the boardwalk that crisp January morning, they were steering clear of this strange bird.

The old woman had directed him to go further down the boardwalk. "It's the Flatbush Day winter fair," she had told him. "They even got the rides runnin' all weekend—so now you can throw up and freeze your buns off at the same time."

Talon had thanked her, left her a well-earned sock for her troubles, then set out alone, braving the cold in nothing more than his Downside shirt and pants. He was quick to find, however, that coats were plentiful on the Topside. One need only to step into the entry of any Topside eatery to find a whole forest of them happily waiting on hooks for whomever happened to need them. Talon found one that fit nicely—a dark, puffy blue thing with a furry hood—then he wandered back to the boardwalk, pleased to find that his coat even came with wads of Topside money in two different pockets!

Now, as he bounded and darted his way along the boardwalk, he had to keep reminding himself that he was not dead, and this was not the Great Beyond—although deep down, a part of him still suspected that it was. Coney Island's winter fair was filled with inexplicable sights and sounds, from the bells and whistles exploding from a building labeled FUN HOUSE, to a great wheel that slowly revolved. "Wonder Wheel," it was called, and it brought people in little boxes skyward, then back again, for no sensible reason beyond the mere joy of doing it. There was a spinning machine of many arms that whipped people around like an eggbeater. Talon watched as people came out stumbling, laughing, and holding one another before running off to ride some other spinning, shaking, racing wonder.

And then there was the Cyclone.

The Cyclone was a white wooden beast that was labeled THE WORLD'S MOST FAMOUS ROLLER COASTER in commanding red letters.

Talon stood before it, transfixed by the mighty contraption as it carried a trainload of riders clicketty-clack to a dizzying height, only to be launched on a wicked, vicious run that left them rattled and giddy. It was strange to Talon, who was used to trains racing single-mindedly toward their destinations, that this little train didn't actually *go* anywhere.

"Three bucks a pop—get your ticket here," said a gruff man in a peeling white booth.

Although a Downsider never shrinks from the roar of a train, this one was far more intimidating than any subway. Talon had no true desire to ride it, but he chose to anyway, if only to spite that Downside voice of warning that still played within his head.

Talon watched the World's Most Famous Roller Coaster three times, not wanting to buy his ticket until he was convinced that the rickety little train consistently came back—and with the same number of riders that it had started with. Then, when he was convinced that neither death nor dismemberment were an integral part of the ride, he handed his money to the man in the booth, then ran up to join the others racing up the ramp.

The line was short, and before he knew it, Talon found himself barred into a freezing, weatherworn seat, not able to escape.

Beside him sat a kid who spoke a strange gibberish to his friends one row back, then he looked at Talon and spoke in an accent Talon thought he recognized from some of the oldest Downside elders.

"Your first time?" the boy asked.

Talon was surprised that it seemed so obvious. Until today, he had always been good at wearing his emotions on the inside rather than the outside.

"Yes," he told the boy, and asked about the language he spoke.

"It's Russian," the boy said, and explained that it came from a place called, naturally, Russia.

"Is it far from here?" Talon asked.

"Not far enough," answered the boy.

And then, with a jolt, the linked cars of the Cyclone pulled forward, ratchetting up the steep incline. As they rose, Talon could finally see the boundless scope of this realm of the sun. He realized that Coney Island wasn't an island at all; it was just part of the Brooklyn expanse. Through the jagged brush of the winter-bare trees stretched row after row of redbrick homes, intersected by a grid of Topside streets. They vanished into the distance, where far-off towers glistened, dwarfing everything in their magnificent shadow. That, Talon knew, must have been Manhattan. Those were the very towers he had peered at from beneath the city's grates, but never had he seen them from such a vantage point. How, he wondered, could they puncture the sky as they did, and yet not tear the sky down?

So many questions filled him now. Too many to consider—but suddenly all those questions were swept away as the coaster cleared the top, and was sent hurtling down that first screaming, insane drop. And in that moment, all past and future vanished for Talon, replaced by a here-and-now that exploded through every nerve in his body. Fear, joy, wind, and wonder had all laid claim to him, and by the time he came to the second drop, any resistance he had was gone. Now he held up his hands like the Russian boy beside him, surrendering himself to the thrill of the ride.

■　■　■

To say that Lindsay's life changed because of her jaunt to the Downside was an understatement. It was an event that touched her very core—discovering such a rich and magical place just a few short strata beneath her feet opened up a universe of possibilities. If such a place could exist in the shadows of a sunlit world, then what else might be possible? Her trip to the Downside drew a pall over the ordinary things in her life.

For the first few days after her Downside excursion, Lindsay was the talk of Icharus Academy—not because she told them anything, but because she didn't. Becky Peckerling, in her own inimitable way, quickly spread the word that Lindsay Matthias had, without warning, crawled into a drain and vanished for an extended period of time. This was high-grade grist for the gossip mill, and in less than two days people were whispering and giggling in her wake through every hallway. She let her hair go wild and took to wearing the ruby earring Talon had given her. Her classmate, Ralphy Sherman, put forth the claim that she was a long-lost Albanian princess, and that the earring was all that remained of the crown jewels.

Rather than be bothered by all this, Lindsay enjoyed it—for the more gossip and speculation they milled, the more separate from them Lindsay felt, as if she had ascended to a more enlightened plane.

By Friday, Lindsay had officially entered the ranks of prep-school freakdom. She even began to attract the *really* spooky kids at school: girls with so many pierced body parts, they looked like human voodoo dolls, and boys who dressed in black and carried around copies of *The Catcher in the Rye.*

But she was not one of *them,* either, and she began to wonder if there could ever be anyone or anything Topside that could pique her interest anymore. Instead, her thoughts were always drawn back to Talon and his peculiar world. She longed to see him again, explore with him. He filled many of her daydreams. Lindsay realized, had Talon been a Topside boy, they probably would have been snared in that hopelessly nerve-racking Topside ritual called "dating." But they were already beyond that particular brand of awkwardness. To Lindsay, holding hands while stumbling through a dark sewer seemed far more natural than holding hands in a dark movie theater. Of course it was a sentiment she couldn't share with anyone else she knew. They simply wouldn't understand.

Yet, even though she wanted to lose herself in the magic

NEAL SHUSTERMAN

of the Downside, and accept the marvelous sights without question, there was a part of her that knew that magic was only sleight of hand. Behind everything was that nagging question of *how?*

How could the Downside have come to be?

The old man Talon had taken her to—The Champ—knew something. The name of a forgotten inventor. But Lindsay put those thoughts aside, not yet willing to dispel the magic of Talon's world.

"I'd like to take a walk today," Lindsay told Todd as they stepped out of school on Friday, "and get to know the city a little better." For three days, according to their father's wishes, Lindsay dutifully returned home from school with Todd, and each day, he complained in an endless harangue about how having to baby-sit her had ruined his life and made the world a lesser place. Her desire to seek out Talon and the Downside grew with each day. All she wanted was an afternoon free from Todd's oppressive thumb to prod the niches where no one went, in search of entry to that elusive place. "Just a few hours by myself…"

"Out of the question," said Todd. Then he added, "If it's so important to you, you can ask Dad's permission when you get home—that is, if he answers his page."

But chances were, he wouldn't answer his page. He claimed to be at a crucial part in his big project, and since her fateful return from her late-night adventure, her father would leave for work before Lindsay awoke and come home after she had gone to bed. Lindsay wondered if the work was really that demanding or was it just an excuse to avoid dealing with her?

"He's sorry you came to live here," Todd told her. "He thinks you're a freak, just like everyone else."

And although most of the things Todd said could easily be deflected, this one hit her hard, because she knew that it might have been just the tiniest bit true.

As it turned out, it was a good thing Lindsay went straight home today, because the package waiting at her front door was far more interesting than anything else in the city.

■ ■ ■

When Lindsay and Todd got home, there was a bum sleeping on their stoop, wearing a bulbous Gortex parka, with the fur hood zipped all the way up, like an Eskimo.

"Oh, great," said Todd. "What is this, the Stoop of the Damned? Y'know, someone oughta invent a bum-zapper. They come up to your door, and ZZZZT!—they're fried!" Todd roused him awake with a rough shake of the shoulder, and the vagrant quickly got to his feet. "Move it, pal, this is private property!"

Lindsay realized who this "bum" was by the way he moved, even before she caught sight of his face nestled within the shadows of the hood. It was the one time Lindsay was thankful for the fact that Todd saw the same basic face on all of the city's homeless, and didn't bother to look at this one any closer.

Talon turned to Lindsay and opened his mouth to speak, but she quickly cut him off. "Charlie!" she said. "I almost didn't recognize you!"

"Huh?" said Talon.

She turned to Todd. "This is Charlie, from my math class.

I took notes for him today, on account of he was...under the weather, right, Charlie?"

"Huh?" said Talon.

"*Gesundheit,*" said Lindsay. She grabbed him with one hand, and with the other quickly turned the key in the lock. "Why don't you come inside?"

She barged past Todd and to the stairs, with Talon in tow. "Come on up, Charlie, and I'll give you the notes."

"Dad won't like you having a boy in your room," warned Todd, but Lindsay already heard the TV on in the living room, which meant that Todd wasn't going to push it. She ignored him, and spirited Talon up the stairs.

"I rode the Cyclone!" Talon said cheerfully.

"Shh!" They hurried down the second-floor hallway, but instead of going into her room, she took them over the threshold between the two conjoined buildings and up another flight of stairs to the gutted third floor of her father's newly acquired brownstone—a mess of molting plaster and wires that twisted like snakes through holes in the walls where the fixtures should be. Only here, as far away from Todd as possible, did Lindsay feel safe enough to talk. "What are you doing? Are you nuts?"

"I rode the Cyclone!" he said again. "And I took a taxi, and I rode in a ferry-ship, and I stood in the face of the great green lady, and I ate a paternity-on-rye!"

Lindsay's head began to swim, and she couldn't help but laugh. "Slow down...you're telling me you've been Topside?"

Talon was like an anxious puppy, practically bouncing off the unfinished walls. "For two days now!"

"But…but what about the Downside? What about the rules?"

"They can stick their rules where the sun don't shine," he told her. And then he proudly added, "The driver of the taxi taught me that one!"

Talon went on to tell her about his first sight of the ocean, and the old woman who had helped him. He told her how, when night had fallen, he took refuge. "The street-beds in the park were too cold," he said, "so I found a green-room that wasn't being used."

"Green-room?"

"You know: square, wheels on the bottom—"

"A Dumpster? You slept in a Dumpster?!"

He smiled, proudly repeating the word: "Dumpster. Yes! It was good, because I could see the moon—did you know that it's sometimes round instead of curved?"

She laughed. "It only looks curved when part of it is in the dark."

She could see him reeling as he tried to absorb the information, as he must have absorbed everything else over these past few days. In the brief time Lindsay had known him, she had never seen him act like this—he was always in such stiff control, rigidly reflecting the Downside way. It both tickled and troubled her that a few days Topside could change so much about him. She wasn't sure which Talon she liked more—the stoic, self-assured Talon who knew his way in the dark, or the wide-eyed boy who made sleeping in a Dumpster sound like a night in paradise.

Although Lindsay could not know it, this truly was the first time in Talon's life he had ever let his emotions take

NEAL SHUSTERMAN

flight. It was Talon's choice not to tell her about his ejection from the Downside, for shame had no place in his life now. So he paced the room, speaking in rapid, shotgun speech, like a Topsider. He barely recognized his own voice, and he liked that. There was that other voice, however, still deep in his thoughts, reminding him of the Downside's golden rule—that the two worlds must never come into contact—but here he was; the two worlds had touched and they had not been destroyed. So who was wiser now: he, or the Advisors who had sent him on a one-way trip to Coney Island?

At last all his wild ranting left him out of breath and light-headed from his own excitement, and as they stood there, grinning dumbly at one another, it seemed that the many walls that had once been between them were gone, leaving nothing but empty space to be filled. So Talon stepped forward and put his hands on her shoulders. "I want to know what you know, Lindsay—see what you've seen. I want you to show me everything there is to see on the Topside."

She laughed. "That'll take an awfully long time."

He pointed down to the Rolex on his ankle. "Time is of low importance."

Then, finally, he broke the last Downside rule left to break. The one rule he wanted to break more than any other.

Even though she was a Topsider.

Even though no one had given approval.

Even though his mother still knew him.

Talon leaned across the space between them, and stole a

kiss...and before long, he realized that Lindsay was more than happy to steal it right back.

Whether or not it was the perfect kiss, neither could say, because neither had experienced any other to compare. But it must have been close, for in that moment something fell into place, and for the first time in either of their lives there was no doubt that everything was now right with the world.

■ ■ ■

Meanwhile, not too far away, work on the Westside Aqueduct's primary shaft had reached a fever pitch. The project was three months behind schedule—of course it had been three months behind schedule last week as well—but Mark Matthias, the bigwig city planner whose project this was, had just about gone ballistic this week, for reasons unknown. He came down hard on the foreman, who came down hard on his workers.

The result was a frenzied speedup.

Dirt and pulverized bedrock was hauled from the thirty-foot-wide hole as quickly as the crane could haul it up, and it was all loaded into an endless stream of dump trucks that would drive up to the edge of the gaping hole to receive their load.

What no one knew was that Mark Matthias's mind was not on his work. In fact, his harsh attitude had little to do with the aqueduct, and more to do with his daughter and her unusual behavior. It would be fair to say that if Lindsay hadn't traveled to the Downside, driving her father to distraction, things would have happened much differently...

...because, had the workers not fallen victim to Mark

Matthias's personal frustration, then maybe that dump truck wouldn't have lurched so recklessly forward to receive its load of rock....

. . .

There was only one person in the Brass Junction today. A faller. One who had not yet been named. A faller who had once held the Topside name of Robert Gunderson. He stood on a scaffold, happily cementing old subway tokens to the ceiling, repairing the various spots where the tokens had come loose. He sang to himself, enjoying the way his voice resonated and filled the solemn chamber. He had reason to sing: In just a few short weeks, he had gained respect for himself and his work. He was appreciated here, and that was more than he could say for the world he had left. This great resurrection of hope was almost enough to outweigh the sorrow he felt at hearing of Talon's execution. Railborn, he was told, would take over the task of naming him—and it didn't thrill the faller one bit, because he had heard that Railborn was partial to the name Flake since they had found him during a snowstorm.

While he pondered a life being known as Flake, there came a vibration from high above. He had grown used to the many groans, echoes, and vibrations that rang through the Downside, the way one grew used to crickets and the rustling of leaves in the countryside—so he didn't think much of it, at first. But as the rumble grew louder, he began to feel concerned—because the tokens were beginning to drop from the roof all around him, tinkling on the floor.

With growing unease, he began to climb down the scaffold, sensing a sudden and all-too-literal "gravity" to the situation that he could not explain—until a moment later, when the dome above him exploded with a massive crash of shattering stone, destroying the scaffold and hurling him to the ground in a shower of stone and tokens.

Dazed from his fall, he dragged himself out from under the debris and sat up, peering through the settling dust. It took a full minute of staring at the sight before him before he could convince himself that this was truly what it appeared to be.

There, lying in the center of the Brass Junction, was the crushed remains of a huge yellow dump truck that had somehow pierced the Downside like a missile. It lay there, now a barely recognizable hunk of twisted metal—and far above, through the gaping hole in the Brass Junction ceiling, came the distant hint of daylight.

Without a moment to lose, he took the closest tunnel and raced off to tell the Wise Advisors of this disaster, and that the unspeakable had happened. A hole had been torn in the World.

12

The Null Tunnel

Had the Great Shaft Disaster been your typical big-city catastrophe, it would have been in and out of the news in a single day, a few heads would roll, and the city would move on. But the discovery of an unmapped chamber beneath the aqueduct shaft made it more newsworthy—and reports that the chamber was paved with fifty-year-old subway tokens erased any doubt as to the nature of this event. This was no catastrophe at all—it was a major archaeological find!

In a few short hours, Mark Matthias went from an unknown civil engineer to an urban Indiana Jones, heralded by the media as the discoverer of some lost world.

Work on the shaft immediately ceased, and the top archaeologists and historians were called in from NYU and Columbia University to examine the site. They were quick to discover that this chamber was actually the junction of two intersecting tunnels—and furthermore, sonic resonant testing revealed a Big Old Tunnel that ran somewhere beneath the mysterious chamber's floor. Reports were made, more experts were consulted, and what began as a construction accident evolved into a full-fledged expedition into the unknown, its spin reversed from tragedy to fortuity.

Through all of this Talon watched in horror, his eyes glued to the images on the Matthias's living-room television that night. As he was not accustomed to jarring cuts from one image to another, it made the whole thing seem all the more nightmarish.

This, thought Talon, as he watched the first team of academics descend into the shaft, must have been how The Champ felt at Pearl Harbor—this most certainly heralded what would soon be a full-scale war.

Talon had no need to hide in the Matthias home now, because Todd, sensing that his father had suddenly become important, rushed to his side as a show of support, but mostly to bask in his unexpected limelight. This left Lindsay and Talon alone to view the unfolding events.

"This is my fault," Talon muttered over and over again.

"How can you say that? You weren't even there," reminded Lindsay. She stood beside him, but each time she tried to get close, he paced to another corner of the room.

"I broke the law," he declared. "The Fates brought me to the Topside to test me. I failed the test, and now the worlds will end."

"That's stupid superstitious nonsense!" snapped Lindsay. "Look around you. Think about the things you've seen—the places you've been over the past few days. Do you really think it's all going to end just because we found the Downside?"

     NEAL SHUSTERMAN

Talon pondered this well, weighing the old prophecy with the new perspective these few days in the sun had granted him. "You're right," Talon admitted. "Your world will survive." He glanced at the TV, where they interviewed Lindsay's father yet again, his words and expressions so exact that Talon began to wonder if they had actually captured time and were playing the same thing over and over and over.

"*Your* world will survive," he said again. "But mine will not."

He was out the door not a second later, without taking as much as his Topside parka to protect him from the unforgiving cold.

■　■　■

Lindsay could have let him go.

She could have stood there in her warm living room, blaming her father and his miserable aqueduct. She could have thrown up her hands, pretending that this was all above and beyond her. It would have been so easy to stave off making up her mind until it was too late to do anything about it. But she cared too much about Talon and the Downside to allow either his superstitious beliefs or her own rationalizations to corner her into inaction. Nobody's world was going to end just because of a falling dump truck, and Talon was not going to disappear into some hole, out of her life again.

Wasting no time, she took to the street after him.

He was not hard to find. As surefootedly as he moved in the Downside shadows, he was as clumsy as an ox when it came to negotiating Topside streets. He smashed his shin on a fire hydrant, and skidded in something a neighbor's dog left on the sidewalk. It slowed him down enough for her to catch up with him just as he reached the corner and leaped into the darkness of a subway station. She followed him down.

"Talon! Talon, wait!"

If he heard her, he didn't acknowledge it. She saw him run into a turnstile, but since he had no token, it didn't budge, and he flipped awkwardly over the bar. But he barely lost momentum, and she found herself losing time as she crawled beneath the turnstile bar rather than search for a token.

He raced to the end of the station, his feet pounding on the yellow caution line at the edge of the platform. Then he leaped off, and disappeared down the tunnel.

Lindsay hesitated, but only for a moment. He had entered the High Perimeter. Well, perhaps he knew how to move through these dark places, but her determination had to count for something. She jumped from the platform, stumbled on the wet, muck-filled ground between the rails, then took off into the darkness, ripping off her coat, trying to feel the air around her with the fine hairs of her arms.

Five minutes later, at the end of her breath, she stopped. The tunnel was absolute pitch-black now. She turned to the left and right, listening to the dead air around her, fearing Talon had taken off down some other connecting tunnel, or worse, found a doorway that led him back to the Downside. She listened for his footfalls, but all she heard was the distant rumble of countless trains racing beneath the city.

NEAL SHUSTERMAN

"Talon, I'm not letting you run away—do you hear me?"

No answer. And then, in a moment, she realized that she had lost track of which direction she had come, or which direction she faced.

"Talon?"

The fear hit her then, petrifying her in this darkness between worlds. *I am alone and lost in a place where sane people don't go.* She took a step forward, then stopped. The third rail. Was it off to her right, or left? In the subway stations, that lethal electrified rail was covered by a protective sheath, should some idiot happen to leap to the tracks, but here in the deep, intestinal maze of the subway lines, no protection was provided. Here, one misplaced footfall could be her last.

She reached her hands forward, and they met with rough stone. She still would not move her feet. Then the air pressure around her began to change. She could feel her ears threatening to pop, the way they did in an airplane or fast elevator. And with the change in air pressure came a rumble, and a faint light from far off.

She didn't need to be told what that meant.

As the light increased, she thought it might help her get her bearings long enough to find a way out of the path of the approaching train, but what she saw in the tunnel around her was even worse than the darkness. This wasn't a wide space filled with many parallel tracks and pillars. This was a single, narrow, black stone tunnel, with a curved roof and no gaps in the stone into which she could crawl. *It's like the inside of a coffin,* thought Lindsay, and the association made her stomach shrivel into a tight little knot.

Now the air began to breeze past her with greater urgency, and the oblique light revealed its source—a pair of headlights coming around a distant bend, lighting the tracks in a shining wedge that led directly to her.

She began to run, cursing her luck, and wondering why it now seemed her lot in life to be trapped in tunnels in the path of deadly things. She ran, praying for the tunnel to open up, or at least provide a doorway or grotto she could hide in, but there was nothing but the dead black walls on either side as the light grew around her, making the tip of her long, ghostly shadow fall thirty feet away.

The conductor blasted his horn idiotically, as if there was something she could do, and then, just before the train overtook her, she was clipped from the side, and smashed, her back to the wall. At first she thought it was the train itself, but when she looked up, there was a figure before her, pressing her against the wall.

"Don't move," Talon said. "Don't even breathe."

He pressed closer still, spreading his hands against the wall, his fingertips hooked into the tiniest gap between the stones, trying to flatten both their bodies against the unyielding tunnel wall.

The train exploded past them, each car passing with a *WHOOSH—WHOOSH—WHOOSH,* the windows a blur of light just inches away. With her head turned to the side, she could see Talon's fingers splayed and sinewy, gripping that tiny space, fighting the awful underdraft that now tried to tear them from the wall and hurl them beneath the wheels. She felt Talon losing his grip—she felt him falling away. She fell as well, unable to hear her own scream in the roaring tunnel…

…And they both found themselves almost tumbling into the eddies of wind left by the train's passage.

"Don't you Topsiders have the sense to feel the rail for trains before entering a 'Null Tunnel'?"

As the last of the light faded, Lindsay noticed one more thing. The pop-top vest he had worn for as long as she had known him was gone, and there, on the ground were its remnants, shredded and twisted.

"Talon—are you hurt?"

It was dark again, and now she could see neither his state nor the expression on his face. She reached out and felt his shoulder, reaching around to his back. He pulled away…but not before she felt something wet, sticky, and warm. "You're bleeding."

"The train scraped against my back."

"Are you all right?"

"As all right as I need to be." But the answer wasn't too convincing.

He took her hand, as he had done in their first trip through the darkness, and led her to a place where the Null Tunnel opened up once more into a labyrinth of switching tracks and alcoves of high-perimeter grime. She couldn't see it, but now she could feel the difference in the air, and in the sound of their footfalls.

"Don't seek me anymore, Lindsay. Don't even think of me."

There was a finality—a decisiveness—in his voice that

Lindsay found as devastating as the sight of the approaching train had been. "What do you mean? What are you saying?"

"From this moment forward, it must be as if we never met," he told her. "I thought I could leave the Downside and run from the Fates—but look what's happened. The Fates have made their wishes known."

"How do you know?" demanded Lindsay.

"I know, because everything we do together, we do in danger."

She had no response to that, because, in spite of all her protests, she knew exactly what Talon meant. Were "the Fates," as Talon called them, punishing them for their audacity, or were they challenging them to rise above all this? It seemed to Lindsay that the Fates showed different faces, depending on how you looked upon them—but she had no clue which perspective was true anymore. She felt as lost as she had back in the Null Tunnel.

And then something occurred to her. She thought again of The Champ, who knew more about the Downside than he would say. There certainly was more to know, if only Lindsay could uncover it. If she could offer him a truth about himself and his world—if she could dispel his superstitions and fill his ignorance with understanding—there would be no need for him to run from her.

"What if...what if the Downside's not the place you think it is?" she asked Talon. "What if I could find a truth that's not written on the Rune Chambers' walls, and prove that you have every right to come Topside whenever you want?"

"Don't speak of things you know nothing about," he said,

with a touch of indignance in his voice, which reminded her of that bold boy who had come to her house on New Year's Eve.

"But if I could *prove* that there's no reason why Downsiders and Topsiders can't mix—"

"Then our problems would be solved...but you won't find such a truth, because it doesn't exist."

Talon led her to a ladder, lit by a crosshatch of dim light, indicating a grate far above. "Good-bye, Lindsay," he said simply, placing her hand on the rung, and then he disappeared once more into the darkness.

Well, thought Lindsay, as she climbed, *maybe he thinks it's good-bye, but he'll be in for a surprise.* Perhaps Talon saw his own life as a Null Tunnel now—locked on a single course that seemed destined as inescapable. But Lindsay would rescue him from his Downside straight and narrow. She would seek the truth, and it would set them both free.

Countermeasures

In those first few hours after the Brass Junction was breached, the Downsiders did not sit idly by to watch their world be invaded. Rather, they had been quite industrious in booby-trapping the tunnels that led from the Brass Junction. Trip wires were set to open sewer valves on the unsuspecting invaders. Blockades of mortar and cow skulls were built to deter the encroaching Topsiders, who were believed to be of limited intelligence and easily frightened away. But if these tricks failed, more drastic measures would need to be taken, and no one could agree on what those measures should be.

Thus, the benevolent anarchy that had maintained the Downside through this decade without a Most-Beloved was quickly deteriorating into the type of anarchy in which heroes and leaders were forged. The Wise Advisors knew this—unfortunately, they also knew that they themselves would never be mistaken for either heroes or leaders. If they weren't careful, the people would dredge themselves up a champion of their own—an idea wholly indigestible to the Advisors. What they needed was a prechewed candidate, easily swallowed, and less likely to give the Wise Advisors acid indigestion. And so, when people came to them asking what they were doing to end this Topside onslaught, they would tell them they were consulting with young Railborn Skinner, who had some brilliant ideas.

This was news to Railborn, because although he did have some ideas, he had never shared them with the Wise Advisors. For several days now, the Advisors had been lauding his upstanding qualities in public, and inviting him and his family to dine with them each night. Naturally, other Downsiders just assumed that his status in this highest circle had been developing over many months, not just several days. In fact, the Advisors treated him as if they knew him all his life—and when they would call him over to include him in some weighty business, he would turn around, still thinking they must be talking to someone behind him.

"We see great promise in you," they told him, in front of enough witnesses to make it stick. "We always have." Apparently they saw in him a light he often dreamed he possessed, but never seriously believed, and Railborn wasn't about to question their motives or their sincerity.

The result of all this was that friends and acquaintances who had mostly ignored Railborn in the past now stood when he entered a room and made him the center of attention.

Strangers began to ask his advice on matters he knew nothing about. People liked him—*everyone* liked him—and it almost made up for the fact that he hadn't really liked himself much since sending Talon to his death.

But no one knew that he was the one had who squealed on Talon. No one but the Advisors, and they kept it their little secret, holding it over his head like a dark sword.

On that dread day when Talon was sent to final judgment, he and Gutta had rested from their Hunting duties to mourn the passing of their friend. Although Railborn's heart pounded out a heavy beat of guilt, and although he felt sure that the blame of Talon's death shrouded his face like a birth-caul, Gutta never suspected. She cried in his arms that day, and he found himself shamefully grateful that he, Railborn, whom she had always ignored, was now her comfort in this time of despair. But still, he had the undeniable feeling that she would much rather have been crying in Talon's arms over Railborn's death.

He took audience once more with the Fourth Advisor, to bare the guilt that he could bare to no others.

"Your guilt is pointless—be rid of it," the Advisor told him. "What's done is done. Think no more of it. Think only to your future, Railborn, which, I assure you, will be a fine one…as long as you do as we say."

The grin on the Advisor's face spoke volumes to Railborn. He knew that the last Most-Beloved had risen to the position at the age of fourteen, because while an adult could rarely be universally loved, everyone could love the right kid.

And so, when disaster fell from above, destroying the

NEAL SHUSTERMAN

Brass Junction, and the entire Downside prepared to gather for what was perhaps the most important meeting in Downside history, Railborn found himself full of good ideas and poised to be that right kid, in the right place, at the right time. In fact, the Wise Advisors were counting on it.

■ ■ ■

What they were not counting on was the return of Talon Angler, and the tenacious research of a Topside girl.

While Talon haunted the High Perimeter, trying to decide the proper time and trajectory of his reentry into the Downside, Lindsay dove full tilt into detective work.

Lindsay knew that Talon had been browbeaten and hamstrung by the events around him, and so nothing short of a complete enlightenment would turn him around. And then maybe, if it came to it, they could both be emissaries, easing the Downside back into a Topside world.

Her father and Todd had gotten home sometime during the night, and as they ate breakfast that morning, watching the morning news, her father was a bundle of nervous energy. "There's a tunnel down there that seems to run from the tip of Manhattan all the way up through the Bronx," he said, bouncing in his chair like a little kid on a sugar rush.

"I know, I saw it," muttered Lindsay. "Careful of the cows."

But as she expected, her father didn't even hear her. "We don't have to spend fifteen years building an aqueduct! Someone built it for us!"

On the news, they discussed how "unforeseen obstacles" were preventing the excursion from proceeding too quickly.

"Like any other archaeological find, we must proceed slowly and with prudence," said a bespectacled man, who was covered in sludge.

"It might take some time," chimed in her father, "but whatever's down there—we'll find it!"

At school, Lindsay spent her lunch period searching the school's meager library and the Internet for a hint of the elusive Mr. Beach, but ultimately realized that if she was going to find anything, she would have to go to the public library—and not just any old branch, but the big one on Forty-second Street, guarded by those famous granite lions. The hallowed halls of knowledge.

"Not a chance," said Todd as they left school that day. "I'm heading over to the Shaft, to see if they've dug up anything new and exciting. You have to stay home, or come with me."

"What if I do your next term paper for you?"

Todd dished her up a gloating Cheshire grin. "In the spirit of free trade in a global economy, I'm always willing to negotiate."

And that was that. Lindsay bought her freedom, and now was even more determined that if she was to become an indentured servant to Todd, this afternoon would be time well spent.

■ ■ ■

"What is it you're trying to find?" Becky Peckerling asked, hovering around the microfilm machine Lindsay worked on. Although it had been easy to dispense with Todd, it proved a greater challenge to shed Becky, who was eager to report to the rest of the school any new and inexplicable freakish things that Lindsay did. So, while Lindsay spun through endless microfilm of hundred-year-old newspapers, Becky buzzed around her like a moth at a porch light.

"If you told me what you were looking for, maybe I could help."

"I'm looking for Alfred Beach," Lindsay told her.

Becky furrowed her eyebrows. "Is that on Long Island?" she asked, then went into a soliloquy on why Jones Beach was better than Rockaway, unless of course, you were a member of a beach club. It was somewhere during this tirade that Lindsay's eyes locked on a faded microfilm image of a mustached man, and a front-page headline that read "Beach's Wonder Down Under." After almost an hour of searching, it was a thrilling sight, and her heart missed a beat.

"Personally, I don't like the locker rooms at public beaches," continued Becky.

Thinking quickly, Lindsay reached over to a pile of books that had been left by the last person to use the machine, and handed the top one to Becky. "Todd's been looking for this book everywhere—could you check it out for him?"

"Todd?" Becky's eyes peeled like a deer on the interstate. Like so many girls at Icharus Academy, Becky admired Todd from afar—which is really the only way one could admire him. "You want me to check something out for Todd?"

"Yes—in fact, why don't you take it to him at the Aqueduct Shaft? I'll bet he'll really appreciate it."

"You think?"

"I do."

Becky took a deep breath, grabbed the book, and happily pranced off. Lindsay wondered if Becky would even notice that the book she was traveling across town to place in Todd's hands was a volume of Shakespearean love sonnets.

With Becky dispatched, Lindsay leaned in close to the machine and began to read that first article, which led her to another, which led her to another, until she found herself immersed in an intrigue that had begun more than a hundred years before she or Talon were born....

Twenty-Thousand
Leagues Under the Earth

Alfred Ely Beach, one of the founders of *Scientific American* magazine and very possibly the inspiration for Jules Verne's Captain Nemo, was one of the reasons the late 1800s was known as the age of invention. That he was forgotten, while other inventors like Bell and Edison were immortalized, is yet another indication of history's selective memory.

Had history not been so selective, it might more easily recall that Alfred Ely Beach, inventor of the first practical typewriter, the cable car, and the hydraulic tunneling bore, also built the world's first subway beneath the streets of New York City. Beach's Broadway tunnel is as mysterious and bizarre a story as you'll ever hear, not just because it was powered by wind, but because the entire subway was built in total secrecy.

As the story goes, to avoid the corrupt hands of the villainous Mayor "Boss" Tweed, the determined Beach took a cluster of down-and-out workers and transformed them into a corps of night-laborers, stealing secretly into basements in the dead of night for three years to build one of the great wonders of the century.

The fact that no one noticed a tunnel being bored directly beneath their busy feet is not as strange as it may seem. In a city full of eye-popping sights and ear-wrenching sounds, one learns to tune things out, and so the only tunnel the citizens of New York saw during those three years was the comfort of their own tunnel vision.

Early in 1870—the same year that the infamous captain of the *Nautilus* was first seen in print—Alfred Beach opened his subway's first two stations to the world, revealing a feast for the senses and sciences that would have made Nemo proud. The main station was a dazzling, fantastical showplace filled with glittering chandeliers, a grand piano, and a fountain swimming with goldfish. The leather-upholstered pneumatic train shuttled from one end of the hundred-yard tunnel and back, powered by a massive fan that pushed the single cylindrical car on a pulse of air.

The train was an overnight success, and heralded as one of the most important inventions of the age...until the corrupt Powers That Be at city hall stepped in and squashed Alfred Beach's efforts, to punish him for his audacious ingenuity. He was forced to stop digging his tunnels, and the pneumatic train was shut down for good. It didn't take long for the tunnel to disappear beneath Broadway, and for everyone to forget.

Lindsay pored over the faded microfilm articles, more

stunned with each one she read. It was no wonder the city had forgotten the man—the Metropolitan Transit Authority would much rather have pushed a visionary like Alfred Beach under the rug—especially when the 1904 subway, the city's "modern" subway system, was nowhere near as brilliant or as elegant as Beach's pneumatic train.

But as Lindsay read and reread each article on the frustrated engineer's life, she began to get a troubling sense that part of the story was missing....Beach wasn't a man who would simply give up a dream he had dedicated his life to. He *was* like her father—driven to succeed at all costs.

It also struck her that Beach didn't just hire the normal "sandhogs" to dig his tunnel. He had taken in the destitute to do the work. Was that by necessity, or by design?

And then there was the reported date of his death: New Year's Day, 1894. Convenient to die on a day of resolutions and new beginnings.

It came to her then in a blast of revelation so powerful, it frightened her.

What if Beach never stopped building his secret subway?

■ ■ ■

It took an hour for Lindsay to make her way to The Champ's pool shell, her revelation keeping her warm against the cold. Quite simply, she had hit the jackpot.

When she arrived, she was shocked to find that the pool was, indeed, a pool once more. Water gushed from a ruptured pipe into the old shell at a thousand gallons an hour, debris had quickly plugged the drain, and by the time Lindsay arrived, the home that The Champ had labored so many years to build was swimming in six feet of water. Wooden chairs, sofa cushions, and board games floated in the rapidly filling pool, and since The Champ could do nothing about it, he had packed his salvageable belongings into a shopping cart, which he called his "urban mobile home," preparing for an unexpected move.

"Nothing here for me anymore," he said, tying down the overloaded cart with the rope that had once held up his chandelier. "Not unless I grow a pair of gills. I suppose the good Lord's tellin' me it's time to move on. Reckon He don't believe in subtle hints."

Lindsay helped cover the heaping cart with a blanket, and tied down the other end. It bulged so much, the thing looked like a covered wagon. "Where will you go?" Lindsay asked. "Maybe I could help you find a place…"

"Never had trouble finding a place before," The Champ told her. "And each one's been better than the last." But his voice faltered just enough to betray his uncertainty.

"Well," he said, "as you don't have a bathing suit, I suppose you're not here for a swim."

"We need to talk about the Downside," she said.

"Much as I'd love to, I've got more pressing matters," The Champ said, turning to glance back at his flooded "apartment."

"What if I told you I know how the Downside got there?"

The Champ hesitated, but didn't look her in the face. "Really," he said, doing a bad job of pretending he didn't care. "And what did you find out?"

"It was Alfred Ely Beach who built the Downside!" Lindsay announced.

NEAL SHUSTERMAN

The Champ leaned against his shopping cart and crossed his arms. "Figured that out, did you?"

Lindsay paced the edge of the filling pool. "I think he took all the people that no one wanted and put them to work, building a great subway tunnel, deeper, and longer—much longer than the first! Talon called that tunnel 'the Bot,' but it didn't seem much different from Beach's other tunnel."

"Go on," said The Champ.

"It seems to me that a man like Beach wouldn't be satisfied handing his creation over to the city, would he? No—the city had already tried to destroy him...and so he kept it for himself, and for the people who built it!" It made perfect sense to her now, the eccentric inventor choosing to invent a society all his own—a secret place where those who had fallen through the bottom of civilization could find the dignity that the Surface World had stripped from them. Lindsay could almost see the first Downsiders—hundreds of impoverished souls choosing to redeem themselves in a hidden utopia rather than live in Topside despair. She could see them raising their children to fear and despise the Topside—to keep themselves apart. Four short generations was all it took for their true history to be completely replaced by the far prouder Downside myth, that they had always been there, and always would.

"The Downsiders," proclaimed Lindsay, "are just 'fallers' themselves, who fell from the real world and made up a false one."

The Champ took a deep breath, releasing it slowly. "My grandfather used to tell me stories about people who went down there and never came back up. I never believed a word of it until Talon came shimmying out of the drainpipe."

"If you knew, then why haven't you told Talon?"

"Not my place," answered The Champ.

"Of course it's our place," insisted Lindsay. "In fact, it's our responsibility!"

The Champ regarded her, his expression unchanging. "And what would you tell him?"

What would she tell him? Wasn't that obvious? "I'll tell him the truth," she said. "That the Downside is nothing more than a hundred-year-old lie, and they deserve everything the Topside has to offer."

The Champ chuckled ruefully at that. "Make waves, and someone drowns," he said. "I've always believed that. Sure, I've made plenty of waves in my day, but only when someone needed a good drowning." He took a long look at Lindsay. "They've got enough trouble down there now, without you helpin' things along."

"They have a right to know...."

The Champ looked up to the pipe gushing in an endless deluge, then down into the pool where it took away all but the old man's life. Then he coughed and spat onto the cracked tile floor. "Worlds come and go, I suppose," he said with sad resignation. "You want to destroy his, I can't stop you." And with that, the old man kicked open the door and rattled his cart out into the bitter wind.

Who Died
and Left *You*
Most-Beloved?

The Downside mood had condensed into a heavy sweat beading on the brow of every citizen. True, the threat of a Topside invasion had always been there, but the Downsiders had always trusted in "the Order of Things," and that, like the two sides of a coin, one would never intrude upon the other. So it was more than just the Brass Junction that had been wounded by this breach...for if "the Order of Things" did not protect the Downside from this, then what other nightmares might be possible?

No one was sweating more than Railborn Skinner, who knew, when the Wise Advisors called a meeting in the Hall of Action, that his entire future lay in the balance.

Since everyone knew that the Wise Advisors were impressed with his brilliant ideas, he figured it was time he actually *told* them his ideas before the meeting. But they had no interest in hearing them and suggested that now was no time for him to begin critical thinking.

"Yes, but everyone's expecting me to say something really smart."

To which one of the Advisors responded: "Wisdom is knowing when to keep your mouth shut."

This left Railborn with a huge dilemma, because his father's expectations were quite the opposite.

"Think sharp," his father instructed him as they left for the Hall of Action. "Think sharp, and wax impressive—and you'll be on the path to Most-Beloved!"

That his own father was speaking the words aloud made it seem all the more possible. *Most-Beloved.* Dare he even think it? No—it was a notion too big to think about now—too powerful to grasp. So instead he chose to think about Gutta, and how, if he did ascend to Most-Beloved, she would see him as more than just a consolation prize.

■ ■ ■

The old city hall subway station was meant to be the crowning glory of New York City's subway system. Back in 1904, no expense was spared in its creation. Since it was the very end of the line, the station was a large semicircle around which the trains would turn and head back uptown. Problem was, straight train cars don't fare well at curved platforms. It might have worked had the train doors been in the center of each car, where the train actually touched the platform, but the doors opened toward the ends, where travelers were faced with a four-foot broad jump. And so the city hall station, although full of pomp and prestige, was, much like city hall itself, virtually useless. It was shut down, boarded up, trains were rerouted, and the whole station naturally became part of the Downside.

The city hall station—or the "Hall of Action," as it had come to be known—was rarely visited by the Downsiders as it was reserved for only the most auspicious, or dire of occasions. This day certainly fit the bill.

Railborn arrived surrounded by an entourage that practically carried him before them like a banner. The tracks, the platform, and the mezzanine were already jammed with people, and more were arriving from all directions. Five thousand in all. The entire Downside population. Then one by one, the Advisors strode in, fashionably late. They made their way through the crowds, sliding craftily between the cheers of some, and the jeers of others, until they took their place sitting in the high perches of five shoe-shine chairs.

The First Advisor began to speak. She was a well-wrinkled woman, whose powerful voice sliced through the agitated crowd, bringing them down to a murmur. "We have convened," she began, "to seek counsel from the citizenry in how to end this most pernicious Topside incursion."

The First Advisor often used large and mysterious words to dazzle "the citizenry." That, thought Railborn, must have been what his father meant when he said "wax impressive."

"All voices will be heard," continued the First Advisor. "Reasonable, or other."

As Down Folk were not a shy lot when asked for an opinion, there was no shortage of ideas. One faction sought a full-scale war. This was the same contingent that always chose bloodshed as the most efficient solution to any

Downside dispute. They were often referred to as the Killthemalls. Others pleaded for the Topside to be received with open arms—for surely once they experienced Downside life, they would see the error of their ways and would all become fallers. This group was commonly known as the Welcomongers.

Still others suggested that if they just ignored the whole thing, it might go away.

The debate raged, and as things began to degrade into the name-calling portion of the meeting, Railborn took a deep breath and raised his hand.

The Advisors spotted him and looked at one another, none of them wanting to take responsibility for Railborn opening his mouth—but finally the First Advisor acknowledged him.

"The Advisors recognize Railborn Skinner."

Whispers all around. Younger children craned their necks to see.

"Uh…I've been thinking," said Railborn. "I've been thinking…and it seems to me that this Topside implosion—"

"Incursion," corrected someone beside him.

"That this Topside *incursion* shows how ungrateful the Topsiders are for the things we give them. And it's about time we punished them for it."

By now, it had become so quiet, you could hear a rat breathe. The First Advisor leaned forward in her chair, her expression somewhere between curiosity and horror. "Continue."

Railborn swallowed hard and cleared his throat, knowing that this was the moment that divided heroes from fools.

"Electricity, gas, and water," he said. "These things all come to *us* first! It's by our generosity that we let them flow onto the Topside." And then he smiled. "I don't know about you, but I don't feel too generous anymore."

There was a moment of silence as the suggestion began to sink in. And then, to Railborn's amazement, it came back to him in a rising crescendo of enthusiasm that not even the Wise Advisors could contain.

"I can blow out the main transformer relays," shouted the master electrical tapper.

"Give me ten workers, and I can have the gas shut down in a day," cried the master gas tapper.

"Heck, why not plug up the sewer lines, too!" said one of the Sludgeman brothers.

It was, quite simply, the solution to appease everyone. The Killthemalls were pleased because it was a war of sorts, and the Welcomongers accepted it because it would teach the Topside the error of their ways without bloodshed. Perhaps the Wise Advisors were right: Maybe he did have brilliant ideas after all—and how perceptive of them to know!

Railborn found himself assaulted by handshakes and slaps on the back while the Advisors all looked to one another, each now wanting to claim responsibility for Railborn opening his mouth.

Railborn was propelled forward amidst hearty cheers toward the Wise Advisors shoe-shine risers.

"Well done, Railborn," said the Fourth Advisor, embracing him. Then he whispered in Railborn's ear, "The next time you have an idea, warn us."

"Do I know that boy?" he heard his mother quip from somewhere in the crowd. "I don't think so!" And that brought applause and a round of laughter, for everyone knew what that meant. Railborn sought out Gutta in the crowd and winked at her.

It was a moment of legend—the kind of legend that fills whole walls in rune chambers—but moments have a way of fizzling just as quickly as they flare. Especially when a ghost arrives to quench the flame.

"I've seen the Topside!" shouted a voice from the back of the station.

People turned to see who spoke, and a woman released a shrill scream that was not at all in the spirit of the moment. But she had a good reason for screaming...for the dissenting voice belonged to Talon Angler, who had just returned from the dead.

It only took a fraction of a second for the attention that had been so freely lavished upon Railborn to shift away from him completely. All heads turned, and the hall erupted with cries of shock, surprise, and even terror.

"It can't be!" The First Advisor fell from her perch and had to be helped up.

Talon's parents nearly trampled everyone in their path to get to him, and most everyone else backed away.

He looked like one would expect after having been dead: His hair was unkempt, his eyes careworn, and he walked as if every step took the full measure of his will. His shirt was torn, and his back was badly bloodied, as if he had been brutally beaten in the land of the dead.

For Railborn it was a dream come true, woven with his

darkest nightmare. First came the shock at seeing Talon, followed by a brief moment of joy that was quickly killed by a burst of overwhelming horror…for Railborn knew that spirits did not return from the dead lightly. Talon must have returned from beyond the pipe to accuse him before the whole Downside, and lay bare his betrayal. Weak, with the world spinning around him, Railborn would have fallen to his knees and confessed, had not the Fourth Advisor firmly grasped his shoulder.

"Wisdom in silence," the old man whispered—but Railborn could hear a quiver of fear in his voice as well. Railborn watched as Talon was embraced by his weeping, disbelieving parents, and then watched as Gutta pushed through the crowd, moving away from Railborn and toward Talon, as she always had—and in that moment, Railborn knew that his own future, bright as it had seemed, was being extinguished before his eyes.

Talon, however, did not know Railborn's anguish. He only knew his own—the pain in his back from the train, which had savaged him far more than he was willing to tell Lindsay. And then the weight of all of those eyes on him. The entire Downside.

Gutta grabbed his hands, holding them tightly as if to convince herself he was still flesh and blood. "But…they executed you!" she cried.

"Yeah," he said, squeezing her hands. "Guess I can't even die right."

He gave her a grin, then lost himself in the embraces of his parents and little Pidge, who never believed he was dead anyway. Then he forced himself free from the loving arms encircling him, pushing his way forward to where the Wise Advisors stood with Railborn. Even the Wise Advisors were shaking in their boots, for few things are more dangerous than a dead man who can still tell a tale.

"Your presence here is a surprise to us, Talon," said the First Advisor, her voice far thinner than usual. "Perhaps you can explain it."

Talon looked around at the awed crowds and chose his words wisely. "The Fates saw fit to pull me from the funerary pipe before I reached its destination," he said. "You sent me to be judged in the world beyond. Consider my return as the judgment passed."

Talon paused and looked at Railborn, who stood dumbfounded in the company of the Wise Advisors. Talon offered him a grin. "Hi, Railborn."

Railborn didn't answer—he only stared, aghast.

Talon took a deep breath. He had heard Railborn's plan as he lingered at the back, before making his presence known. A week ago, he would have been the one lifting Railborn on his shoulders, ready to leap into his utility war—but things change. "I've seen a vision of the Topside, Wise Advisor," he said, once more choosing his words with caution.

"What was your vision?" asked the Second Advisor.

"I saw a world that stretches beyond sight. A vast place, with more people than one could count in a lifetime."

"And all of them dependent on us!" shouted Railborn, trying to bring the attention back to his war plan.

Talon pursed his lips and spoke softly to his friend. "Maybe not."

NEAL SHUSTERMAN

Railborn's face hardened, as if he had been struck in the face. "Maybe you've gone over to their side."

"If I had, I wouldn't be here."

"Enough!" shouted the Fourth Advisor, and he turned to the enforcers beside him but spoke loud enough for everyone to hear. "Have the undertaker arrested. Clearly he sabotaged the execution." And then he turned to Railborn.

"Railborn, as man of the hour, we leave it up to you—what shall be done with Talon Angler?"

Talon smiled at him, glad to be left in the hands of his friend, and ready to concede that his return had been easier than he had thought.

But Talon wasn't the only one who had changed over the past few days.

Railborn saw this as a test. A test by the Advisors before the whole Downside, and everything hinged on whether or not he passed it. All his life he had lived in Talon's shadow, and here, again, his time of glory was eclipsed by Talon's unfathomable return from the dead. And even though Talon's return released Railborn from his deep guilt, it also heralded the death of himself as anything more than just Skeet Skinner's unremarkable son. It would all be over, unless he passed this test the Advisors had set before him. There was only one way for him to succeed now.

"This vision of the Topside sounds like the ravings of a lunatic," Railborn finally said. "So I say he belongs in the Chamber of Soft Walls, until his mind returns!"

Talon locked eyes with Railborn, the betrayal now lying naked between them, and as much as Railborn wanted to look away in shame, he didn't. "I'm sorry, Talon," he whispered. This time it was Talon's turn to stare, speechless.

"No!" shouted a voice in the crowd. It was Gutta. She hurled a look at Railborn that went miles beyond disgust, and then dismissed him entirely, pushing her way toward Talon even as the enforcers grabbed him and led him away.

The Fourth Advisor slunk up beside Railborn. "You continue to surprise me," he said, clearly pleased. But it only made Railborn feel all the more empty. It didn't make a difference what he did now, or how the campaign against the Topside went, or even if he rose to Most-Beloved. For he had just lost everything that mattered, and now Railborn knew, even more than Talon, how it felt to die.

16

The Festival of Outages

The next day, the power went out on the island of Manhattan. It happened at noon. Then, two hours later, all gas appliances ceased to function as well—and an hour after that, faucets coughed, sputtered, and gave up the ghost, followed by the phones. By 4:30, people began to notice sewer lines backing up into drains around the city, in spite of the fact that no one was able to flush anymore. Then, by sundown, sensing that the timing would never be so perfect, the garbage men went on strike, putting a rather zesty cherry on top of the city's nightmare sundae.

The only machinery left working was the clockwork of blame, whose heavy hands were all beginning to point toward Mark Matthias.

"Such a massive utility shutdown," concluded the various heads of the various utility bureaucracies, "could only be caused by someone mucking around deep below the surface." And everyone knew who the city's biggest mucker-upper was. Mark Matthias went from urban Indiana Jones to Public Utility Villain faster than you can say, "Help, I'm stuck in the elevator."

Meanwhile, the gas company, phone company, and the Department of Water and Power mobilized every emergency unit they could find to end the crisis, but to no avail...for as soon as the crews would think they had isolated the source of the problem, that source would move elsewhere.

Nothing in the history of the city had so successfully crippled it—but the effect was not what one might expect. While it is well-known that big-city breakdowns often lead to wild looting binges, it's also well-known that New Yorkers hate to be told what to do. Thus, the collective consciousness of the city decided that the looting trend was as passé as last year's fashions. Instead, most chose to see this like a cruise ship stuck on a sandbar. What else is there to do but party?

Warmer weather had moved in, bringing people out into the streets in droves. Supermarkets donated food before it spoiled. Bottled water companies called in their trucks from across the nation, and before long the city had become the single largest block party on record. It was instantly proclaimed "the Festival of Outages" by the mayor, who suggested that the utilities be shut down once every year in the name of conservation and community relations.

That night, Eighty-fourth Street was awash with people cooking up ethnic foods over trash-can barbecues. Todd organized a dance on the Matthias's roof, charging his

NEAL SHUSTERMAN

guests two D batteries for admission, thereby assuring that his portable CD player would never run out of tunes.

Lindsay observed all of this with a wild sense of amusement and the guilty pleasure of knowing something that nobody else did. She instinctively sensed that this utility fiasco was of Downside doing, and she wondered if they had any idea how many millions of people they had successfully inconvenienced.

All the more reason to find her way down there again and to give them the larger perspective of the world that they so needed. With the Brass Junction shattered, and their world exposed to the scrutiny of the sunlit world, they could no longer live in secrecy. They would be forced to shed their ignorance. Lindsay found herself in the unique position to help them through it—both her and Talon. Lindsay fancied herself a missionary, bringing them the light of Heaven in a very literal sense and putting it into Talon's hands. The hard part was finding her way back down, for The Champ's abandoned pool was still full of water, and she didn't dare venture into the subways again, even if the trains weren't running.

When the answer finally came, it struck her with more than a little bit of irony that the threshold of the Downside had been right in front of her nose—but her nose was buried in a microfilm machine.

It was her father who first told her about the curious history of New York City's main library back when she first arrived, in an attempt to dazzle her with a tower of architectural tidbits. The short version of the story was that the library was built on the city's old reservoir, and, like a sidewalk tree, the library's roots extended out unseen beneath the streets.

"There are rooms within rooms within rooms down there," her father had told her. "Places that no one has been for ten, maybe twenty years."

What he was describing, although he didn't know it, was a classic interface to the Downside. And so, while everyone else was dancing in the streets, Lindsay took her folder of century-old news articles, complete with her own theories and extrapolations, and set off for the library.

■ ■ ■

With no electricity, the library was closed, of course, but that also meant that the security systems weren't working and an enterprising person could find a way in.

Turns out, getting in was disappointingly easy. All Lindsay had to do was wait until the posted guard got up to relieve himself in one of the nonfunctioning bathrooms. Lindsay simply slipped in through the front door and, with flashlight in hand and a crowbar in her backpack, descended to the library's lower levels.

Once there, she found a door labeled RESTRICTED ACCESS—AUTHORIZED PERSONNEL ONLY, an invitation if ever there was one. Lindsay stepped through and found that she had entered the catacombs.

There, in the library's decrepit bowels, she had a clear and chilling vision of history decomposing. She found dust-covered shelves and half-opened vaults filled with the knickknacks of ages. Age-old historical letters of great significance. Death masks of renowned poets, and curious objects of unknown origin that someone deemed worthy of cataloging. She wondered if the great library at Alexandria could ever have been so eerily exotic as this place.

She ventured though one open vault door into another, then descended a staircase, its stone steps layered in dust like a gray fall of snow. It was clear that no one had ventured down here since before she was born. She turned the corner and found herself in a hallway with no shelves, and at the very end, a black iron door that looked like none of the others. There was no lock on that door, or more accurately, the one that was there had been worn away by decades of rust. She pushed it open with a squeaking complaint and found herself on a catwalk in a stone space about ten feet high.

This, she thought, must have been left over from the old reservoir. A ladder led her down to a floor flooded in two inches of brackish water, and there on the wall, just above the water level, was a grate breathing a steady flow of warm air that smelled very different from the bitter odor of mildew around her. There was also the far-off sound of children. She had found her entryway!

Ignoring the icy water at her feet, Lindsay pried open the grate with the crowbar, then forced her way through the hole, leaving behind the library bowels and entering the Downside.

Once through the vent-hole, she quickly got to her feet. She didn't need her flashlight anymore. The place was lit well enough to see—apparently electricity still flowed freely down here. She took in her surroundings. This wasn't a place that Talon had shown her. She was looking at an old steam engine, and although it sat on a single piece of track, it was walled in on all sides, leaving only a low doorway for people to come and go.

The train was painted in bright primary colors and was swarming with small children. As soon as they saw her, the games ended and they became quiet, staring in the way small children do when they don't know whether to heed their fear or curiosity.

"Children, go home," said a woman as she came around from the other side of the play-train. Although the woman's hair and clothes were clearly Downside, the look on her face was universal. She moved out in front of the children, ready to do battle with this intruder as the kids funneled out through the low doorway. *Do I really look that dangerous?* Lindsay wondered.

"Go out the way you came," the woman demanded, and then she swallowed, "…or I will have to kill you." But clearly the woman had no weapon, and there was no bite to her threat.

"I mean you no harm," Lindsay said, then rolled her eyeballs at how stilted it sounded. She might as well have said, *"I come in peace. Take me to your leader."*

"Others are coming," threatened the woman. "Leave now."

But Lindsay just took a step closer, and the woman took a step back, maintaining five feet of air space between them. "I can't leave," she said. "I have to speak to Talon. Talon Angler."

The woman's eyes seemed to change at the mention of his name.

"Do you know him?" Lindsay asked.

She didn't answer, but her body language told Lindsay all

NEAL SHUSTERMAN

she needed to know. It was as if Talon's very name was the password. She wondered what had happened when he returned here, that could make the mention of his name have such sway.

"I know it's dangerous," Lindsay pressed, "but it will be more dangerous if I don't see him."

Lindsay waited, and waited a moment more, saying nothing until the woman finally said, "I'll take you to him."

■ ■ ■

Just like anywhere else in the world, the Downside had its less attractive spots. The Chamber of Soft Walls was a nasty cavernous space padded on every side by old mildewed mattresses, and populated by all those considered in their wrong mind.

As Lindsay peered through the barred window, she couldn't help thinking of something she had heard of in history class: an *oubliette,* the forgetting place—a miserable medieval dungeon where offenders too unimportant to torture were thrown in and left to die. Of course, the plates of food and the cleanliness of these Downside prisoners' clothes showed Lindsay that the people here were adequately cared for, but it didn't change the fact that they were put here to be forgotten.

A guard who had been away from his post returned with enough intimidation to make up for his absence. "What business do you have here?" the guard asked with a stern voice.

"None," said the woman who had led Lindsay there. "But *she* does."

The guard scanned Lindsay up and down, quickly reading the foreignness of her clothes. His eyes darted nervously, unprepared for a Topsider in his jurisdiction.

"She's from the Surface," said the woman.

"I can see that," sneered the guard, insulted to be taken for an idiot.

When he turned back to Lindsay, there seemed less fear in his eyes and more hopefulness. Although he must have been in his thirties, he suddenly looked many years younger.

"Are you here to see Talon?" he asked in little more than a whisper.

When Lindsay nodded, he took a step closer. "Is it true the things he says about the Topside?"

Lindsay shrugged. "I don't know what he said."

He nodded as if in some profound understanding, then turned the key in the rusty door and flung it open with a painful arthritic complaint of old metal hinges.

Lindsay took a step toward the door, but before she passed into the Chamber of Soft Walls, the guard stopped her with a beefy hand on her shoulder. "You know," he said, "not all of us want to see Talon in there."

And finally Lindsay understood why she had been allowed to get this far. There was dissent in the Downside—*real* dissent—perhaps for the first time in its history. And Talon was at the center of it.

Lindsay took a deep breath, feeling the sudden weight of a world on her shoulders. Even though that world was not her own, it was still oppressively heavy. She opened her backpack, pulled out the folder of Downside truths she had brought with her, then crossed the threshold.

The cavern was sparsely populated. Apparently not many people were consigned to this soft corner of hell, and Talon was easy to spot. He sat by himself in a far-off corner. She slowly approached him, awkwardly navigating the floor made of wall-to-wall mattresses. It was like walking on a trampoline. Although she was happy to see him, his circumstance and the gravity of her task stole from her the joy she wanted to feel.

Talon looked up to her from where he sat, eating a bowl of stew. His spoon missed a beat, but then he continued.

He won't show me his surprise, she thought, but then she realized that it was more than just surprise. He was hiding his humiliation at being found like this.

"Did they catch you and bring you here," he asked, "or are you 'just visiting'?"

She smiled, catching his meaning right away. *"Just visiting,"* she said. "If you like, I could help you roll doubles to get out."

He refused to return her smile, so she kept her distance.

"How did you get in here?"

"I used my Topsider wiles," she said. "And, besides, you have a lot more friends than you realize."

He sighed bitterly. "Anyone crazy enough to return from the dead doesn't have friends. Just enemies and followers." He put down his bowl of stew. "I don't want either."

Lindsay sat down beside him, leaning back against a padded wall, and waited to see if he would move away. He didn't. "I'm sorry they put you in this place," she told him. "But I've brought something that could get you out. Something important."

Again, he tried to hide his feelings, but his curiosity leaked through the cracks in his facade. "Important to whom?"

"To you…to the guard at the door…to the people who put you in this place. To everyone in the Downside." She could tell when he began to sense how truly important this was. She held the folder out to him, but he made no move to take it.

"I've always believed," she said, "that the truth can fix anything, no matter how messed up things get. Now that the Topside knows you're here, maybe the truth is the only thing that can fix it…make things easier on the Downside."

"The Topside doesn't know we're here," he reminded her. "They've seen some of our works, but they haven't found us."

"But they will."

Talon looked away, not able to deny it. "The others think they can beat the Topside with this utility war, but they can't. The Topsiders will keep digging until they root us out, won't they?"

Lindsay nodded sadly. "There're probably more people working for the Department of Water and Power than your entire population."

Talon turned his eyes upward, and she could see tears forming. "Imagine that," he said. Then he reached out, and for a moment, Lindsay thought he was reaching for her. She would have taken his hand, comforted him, but it was the folder he was reaching for. He grasped it, and Lindsay let it pass from her hands into his.

"Will I like this as much as *The Time Machine*?" he asked.

Lindsay began to feel doubts creep in the moment he took the folder, but she bullied them away. Talon had to be exposed to the truth, and she had to believe it would help more than it would hurt. "Read it," she said. "And we can talk about it afterward."

He looked at the closed folder, then turned to her, not ashamed to let a tear roll down his face. "Thank you, Lindsay."

She leaned forward and kissed him gently on the forehead, but as she moved away and they caught each other's eyes, they both knew that it simply wasn't enough. And so once more they stole from each other a forbidden kiss. This time there were no exploding chambers, no plunging trucks, just the two of them in a dim, padded room two hundred feet beneath the city.

The kiss seemed to be over the moment it started, and when they looked around they noticed they were the center of attention for a handful of crazy and not-so-crazy comrades. Lindsay left quickly, the thought of a long good-bye too painful to bear.

■ ■ ■

She was led back to her point of entry by the same woman, who asked her no questions. Then Lindsay made her way up through the library much more quickly than she had descended. In a few minutes she was out in the waning revelry of the powerless predawn streets, trying to outrun the memory of those last few moments with Talon, and to deny that they had truly said good-bye.

When she arrived home, Todd and her father were predictably absent. Todd was, no doubt, still on the roof, fanning the final embers of his party. Her father was probably out seeking solutions to the utility crisis.

It was as she lay down on her bed, giving in to her exhaustion, that her bully of moral obligation began to lower its fists. In those half-lit moments on the High Perimeter of sleep, Lindsay began to doubt her own motives, and to suspect she had done something profoundly misguided.

■ ■ ■

Once Lindsay was gone, Talon began counting to himself, trying to stave off as long as possible the opening of the folder. She had told him he had a lot of friends, and that frightened Talon more than anything. It made him feel glad to be sheltered from them here in this lonely place. Because who was he, really? Just a pain-in-the-ass kid with more nerve than sense. Who was he to be revered by anyone?

But even here, his fellow lunatics whispered of how he walked into the Hall of Action and humbled the Advisors by his mere presence.

But I didn't return from the dead, he kept insisting to them, and to the people who came to peer at him through the door. *The pipe broke, that's all.*

One of his padded-room peers said the wisest thing of all: "Don't be an imbecile," he had said. "Of course they know you didn't return from the dead...but you *were* on the Topside, and you *did* rattle the Advisors more than anyone ever has. Until you walked in, nobody realized how much the Advisors needed to be rattled, and now folks are longing to see them quiver again."

Perhaps he was right, but did anyone realize how rattled Talon was, too?

Lindsay's folder sat in his hands so tightly now that the sweat of his palms soaked through the cardboard, leaving damp shadows of his fingers. Then, when he could hold out no longer, he flipped open the folder, to impale himself on this truth that Lindsay had so kindly given him.

■ ■ ■

Elsewhere, in too many locations to count, city workers burned the midnight oil trying to isolate the cause of the utility foul-up. When they exhausted all of the usual suspects—transformers, clogged junctions, and such—they had no choice but to go deeper still into crevices and crannies they never would have before dreamed of going. Deep in those unexpected places they found stone walls and impassable barriers that appeared to serve no purpose other than to seal off the corridors and chambers that lay beyond.

"Perhaps," some of the city workers mused, "it's more of those subway-token rooms built by the sewer fairies." That would always get a laugh, because few of them really believed the token-junction existed, in spite of reports, and those who did were convinced it was a single freak occurrence, and no other place like it would ever be found. So, as they began to drill, they had no clue they were about to break through into a world hung with diamonds and dreams.

■ ■ ■

The Downside was aware of every potential point of invasion, and they steeled themselves for the upcoming battle with skin-piercing tin swords, eye-blinding high-beam flashlights, and bottle-shard arrows. They had heard that the Topside was already celebrating in the streets, and they took that to be a very bad omen. Railborn was sent from place to place to boost morale, which was fading fast, as the muffled sound of jackhammers grew louder around them.

It was toward the brookward edge of the world that Railborn found Gutta. She was stationed with a few other kids at one of the safer partitions, where drilling couldn't be heard. When Railborn approached, she turned away.

"I have nothing to say to you," she told him coldly. He had expected that and worse, but he was determined not to be brushed off.

"I had to do what I did," Railborn said. "Talon was about to ruin everything."

"So you decided to ruin everything yourself."

Behind them, Strut Mason and the other kids snickered, but Railborn threw them a glance that shut them up. Railborn turned back to Gutta, hardening his jaw in a display of his leadership qualities. "I don't have to explain my actions to anyone."

He thought she might slug him then. His hands were ready to reach up and catch her arm in midswing, for he knew if she connected, it would hurt like a pole to the jaw. But Gutta was less predictable than she used to be. Instead, she spoke softly enough so the others wouldn't hear. "You sound like your father, and he doesn't impress me."

She walked away from him to the dead-end tunnel up ahead. Railborn followed. "All right then, what *does* impress you?" he asked, now far enough away from the others that their conversation could be private.

She thought about her answer—and the fact that it was well-considered made it all the harder to hear. "The way Talon walked into that crowd—*that* impresses me," she said, "because he wasn't just doing it for himself."

Railborn felt like screaming. He felt like pounding his fist against the wall until it hurt so much, he could stop thinking of Talon. But he didn't. Instead, he stood there and took a deep breath.

"I can be that way," he told her. "I can be that way when I'm Most-Beloved...," but she cut him off with laughter that stung even worse than her words. And just when he thought his frustration was more than he could bear, she reached out and gently touched his face. He wasn't expecting it. He didn't know how to respond. So unpredictable.

"You won't be Most-Beloved, Railborn," she told him with such certainty, hearing it was like swallowing ice. "No one will be."

"Wh-What do you mean?"

"Don't you know?"

Railborn only shook his head.

And so she told him. "Your war didn't work, Railborn," she said. "And now the World is coming to an end."

And then a second later...it did.

■   ■   ■

Silence is not always a good thing. There is silence before a tornado, and the winds are fiercest just outside the tranquil eye of a hurricane. And just because a tunnel is quiet, it doesn't mean that it's safe…because unlike jackhammers or drills, explosives make no noise before they do their damage.

The blast came without warning and blew Railborn back through the tunnel, where he landed hard against the other kids. There was no way for him to know or really understand what had happened—not in the brief time he had to piece together the tattered moment. All he knew was that there was a tremendous ringing in his ears, and blood on his face. Then reality struck him with such force, it made everything else seem insignificant.

Gutta—where was Gutta?

Vessels of the Soul

What dim light there had been in the tunnel had been blown out by the blast, and now a heavy fog of pulverized stone filled the air, making breathing a burden. Railborn pushed his way through the thick dust, stumbling over the rubble, until he fell over something soft that lay unmoving on the ground.

"Gutta? *Gutta!*"

He found her face in the dark and touched her lips, searching for the moist feel of her breath. He put his ear to her chest, listening for a heartbeat, but his own labored breathing made it impossible to hear. When he pulled his ear away, he realized it had become warm and wet, covered with what could only be blood.

Then came the lights—sharp, violating flashlight beams poking and prodding through the huge hole at the end of the tunnel. As the light hit Gutta, he could see the blood that bloomed from her abdomen. Then he heard the voices of men as they moved toward the breach from the other side. The men who had done this to Gutta, babbling to one another of unimportant Topside things—and that's when Railborn snapped.

In that moment, Railborn ceased to be human. No one is quite sure what he became. Perhaps he was suddenly filled with the spirits of all the gators his father had killed, or perhaps he dredged up something even darker, and angrier. It is said that Railborn's war cry could be heard from one end of the Downside to the other, and that if you listened on quiet days, you could hear it echoing still. He lunged through the hole at the invaders, bellowing a cry of rage and anguish beyond the measure of either world. When those workers on the other side heard it, their blood chilled, and their courage turned to cowardice. An instant later, Railborn came through the cloud of dust, a beast covered in gray powder, hurling bricks and stones. The Topside workers turned and ran, dropping their flashlights, stumbling over one another to escape from the beast that wailed.

When they were gone, Railborn crossed back through the breach and returned to Gutta. The fury was released from him, leaving behind panic and desperation. He knelt beside her and, in the light of the fallen flashlights, he saw the sharp wedge of stone that had punctured her belly like a stake—but now he could see her eyes fluttering with the faintest sign of life. She was still alive...but barely.

The others stood around her, too frightened of the sight to get close. "We'll get her to the healers," Strut Mason weakly suggested.

NEAL SHUSTERMAN

Railborn knew that would be useless. The healers had herbs for many things, and they were skilled in the sewing of wounds—but those were always surface wounds...and there was a saying among healers: *A wound that touches the Downside of the flesh breaks the vessel of the soul.*

"Hurry," insisted Strut. "My uncle is healer to the Advisors—there's no one better!"

But Railborn already knew what the healer would tell him. *Let her soul spill free from its broken vessel,* the healer would say. *Accept that which cannot be mended—you have no choice.*

But he did have a choice. It was an unthinkable choice that he never thought he'd consider...but he forced himself to consider it now. As every Downsider knew, Topsiders were cheaters of the highest order. They lived their ignoble Surface ways, and were so skilled at deception that they had learned to cheat death itself. Sometimes with potions and pills, and other times with brazen sleight of hand in Topside hospitals. Of course, those were all stories—but Railborn was wise enough to know that at least some of the stories must have been true.

Railborn lifted Gutta in arms that had grown strong from a lifetime of the rough play of a hunter's son. Then he turned toward the hole.

"Where are you going?" shouted Strut. "That's the wrong way!"

But Railborn didn't answer him and didn't turn back, for fear that he might change his mind. With Gutta pressed tightly against him to stem off her flow of blood, Railborn stepped over the breach and into the world he so despised.

The sentry who guarded the Chamber of Soft Walls did not know what the Topside girl had left for Talon—only that it brought Talon to the very state of madness he had been accused of. The guard watched through the little window in the door as Talon buried his head in his hands and wept, then hurled the pages across the room only to gather them back again, on his hands and knees, chasing away any other inmates who tried to look at them. Finally, with the papers collected, Talon stood and strode to the door.

The guard, who had never been intimidated by anyone, felt a wave of fear ricochet through him and settle in his knees, which began to shake.

"I wish to be released now," was all Talon said.

The guard stammered, grasping for a way to answer him. How do you say "no" to the one whom the Fates had deemed worthy to survive an execution? How do you refuse the one whom even the Wise Advisors feared?

"I can't do that," the guard said apologetically.

Talon waited, his eyes bloodshot and worn. Then he said again, "I wish to be released now."

As much as the guard wanted to go down in history as being the one who set Talon Angler free, his sense of duty was strong. "I'm sorry. I can't."

Talon was unrelenting. This time he asked, "Is the war going as expected?"

The guard looked away. There was no denying that the Topside was much more formidable an enemy than expected. They had forces amassed all around the Downside now. It was only a matter of time until they broke through, and presumably enslaved them all. "No," the guard told him. "It is not."

"And do the Advisors have a plan for when the walls fall?" Talon asked.

Again, the guard could not look him in the eye. Word was that the Advisors were collecting their belongings, preparing for an escape, as if there were somewhere they could run. "No," he told Talon. "They have no plan."

Talon nodded, and said again, "I wish to be released now."

This time the guard swung the door open wide, and left it that way as he ran off to join his family in these last hours of the World.

■　■　■

In the city high above, the morning sun shone through a cloudless winter sky, assaulting streets that were eerily vacant. Last night the spirit of the city had risen like a bullet shot into the air, but now that bullet had reached its peak, hanging there in the silence of the morning, ready to fall with lethal gravity. No power, no water, no gas. Nothing to do but wait.

There was, however, a building on First Avenue that existed like an island in the city. It had its own generator and massive cisterns that still flowed long after most others in the city had run dry. The place functioned because it simply *had* to function.

It was to this place that Railborn carried Gutta, for although he liked to deny any knowledge of the Topside, he knew from his Catching rotation that Topsiders brought their dying in screaming white cars to this place—this "hospital"—although he couldn't fathom why it would be called that, as it was as inhospitable a place as he had ever seen.

He had risen from a forgotten cellar onto the early morning street, Gutta a limp weight in his arms. Ignoring his terror of the open sky, he forged through the sunlight and the midwinter chill that seeped through the pores of his skin like a disease. With his eyes locked straight ahead of him, he ran toward his destination.

Once through the hospital's doors, action had been quick. Gutta was taken from him and spirited off on a rolling table while a healer asked him what had happened.

"It was the war," Railborn told him, but the healer had looked at him with uncomprehending eyes.

"What war?"

It was then Railborn finally began to realize how very different this world's perceptions were from his own.

Through a slit in a swinging door, Railborn watched in unblinking terror as a gaggle of green-clad healers worked on Gutta, prodding her with pins and tubes, bringing sacks of blood, hooking her up to inconceivable devices, and performing acts on her that seemed more like torture than healing. Railborn held his tongue, for he knew that the cheating of death must be a complicated matter.

Then they questioned him—but he was careful only to tell them what they needed to know: that he and Gutta were here on their own and completely alone in this world; that they had no money, no belongings; that they came from "another place," which he refused to identify; and that their very existence would not have been recorded.

That was hours ago.

Now he stood at the threshold of the room where they had placed her, afraid to see what they had done to her. He ventured into the room to find Gutta asleep on an elaborate mechanical bed, still beneath a siege of tubes and strange devices. It made Railborn think of the old fairy tale: the beauty asleep in a deep cavern of thorns. Only the kiss of a Most-Beloved would awaken her—but he didn't dare kiss her for fear that she might slap him silly, even in this state.

As he stood there, a woman entered and identified herself as a social worker. "I've been assigned your case," she told him, and Railborn nodded, neither understanding nor caring what she was talking about.

"Will she live?" Railborn asked—a question he had asked everyone, and which no one was willing to answer.

"I'm not a doctor," the woman said. "But her condition is stable. I think she'll be okay."

Railborn heaved his relief so heavily from his shoulders that he became light-headed and needed to grab the wall for support. Then, with that burden finally lifted, he dared to ask himself the question he had been avoiding since first setting foot on the Topside: *So what happens now?*

The woman looked at his Downside clothes, heavily stained with Gutta's blood, and held out to him a set of the green garments the healers had worn. "You'll have to take those clothes off," she said.

Railborn raised his chin and looked into this woman's eyes, realizing what she was requesting. Railborn accepted it as a call to duty.

"I understand," he told her. Then, taking the clothes from

her, he stepped into the small bathroom, closing the door behind him.

There were rules for how a Downsider lived. They were clear and simple, always stated in black and white—and even when breaking those rules, Railborn knew there were rules for the proper way to break them. Standing before the bathroom mirror, Railborn peeled off his Downside garments until he was standing as naked as the day he was born. Then he began to intone the pledge.

"I have climbed through the roof of the World…" he began, his eyes fixed on his reflection, "and I now renounce the Downside, and the life I had led…"

There was a balance, Railborn knew. Nothing was achieved without loss. Without sacrifice.

"…I shed all the ties that held me there…"

Gutta's life was not a gift but an exchange—a bargain for which he now had to pay.

"…I take nothing with me but my flesh. Even my name I leave behind…"

He flicked away a tear that had no business being there, now or ever.

"…and I swear never to seek the Downside again, for as long as I live."

With the incantation complete, Railborn stood silent, locked on his own eyes in the mirror—wide, dark pupils that would soon close to pinpricks in the bright light of day he and Gutta would now live in. Stripped of everything he had been, Railborn finally felt worthy to become the Most-Beloved he now would never be…but as he dressed himself in the Topside clothes and prepared to receive his new life, he knew in his heart that if he could be Gutta's most-beloved in this strange, uncovered world...it would be enough.

■ ■ ■

Like Railborn, there was no question in Talon's mind as to what he had to do. He left the Chamber of Soft Walls knowing his destination. He did not want to be noticed, so he kept to the darkest Downside corridors, navigating as he often did by the feel of the air around him. In the silence of those dim passageways he thought once more about Lindsay, and the revelations she had inflicted upon him.

When he had viewed the reports Lindsay had compiled for him, it was as if the bottom had dropped out of his soul. If it were all true, then everything he believed about himself and his world was a lie. And yet, even as he felt his sense of place and purpose disintegrating into that bottomless pit, he felt a new sense of purpose rising to take its place—taking the fragments that Lindsay had shattered and re-forming them into something stronger than before. When Talon had risen to demand his release from the Chamber of Soft Walls, he had felt numbed by this heightened sense of purpose—elevated so high, he knew the guard could not refuse him. Now as he walked in the dark, he wondered if he was merely in some sort of shock, or if everything in his life truly was falling into place. He felt heat before him now, the temperature climbing a degree with every step, until at last he could see the flickering flame and the long stairway descending ahead of him.

There was only one place he could go now—he had

known it from the moment he read the first pages about the wayward Topside inventor. But knowing where he had to go didn't mean he was ready for the burden—and even though he had already faced death by water, it didn't make it any easier to face death by fire in the one place that no living Downsider had ever seen. The most sacred and mysterious spot there was. The Place of First Runes.

He reached the bottom of the stairs and saw exactly what he was always told he would see: two steadfast sentries, and beyond them a passageway of flame. The two sentries were not the type that could be easily swayed to allow passage. They held electrified swords that were wired to a high-voltage line dangling from the ceiling. The floor of the passageway behind them was of porous pumice that was continually pumped with gas and set aflame. One sentry had the key to turn off the flaming floor, and the other was trained to kill him if he tried.

Talon approached the sentries, the passageway around him as hot as an oven and flickering with the blue gaslight. The sentries were dressed in heavy ceremonial uniforms forged from only the finest cloth fragments. They were drenched in sweat, partially from the heat of the flames behind them and partially from the anxiety of holding those lethal electrified swords in their rubber-gloved hands. They gripped those swords more tightly as Talon approached. He stopped just short of striking distance.

"I suppose you know who I am," he said, hoping he could wield his reputation as well as they wielded their swords.

"We don't care," said one of the Rune Sentries. "If you take one step closer, we will kill you."

Talon showed them the folder that Lindsay had given him. "These are First Runes," he told them. "I must be allowed in."

"Impossible," said the other sentry. "If they're not already in there, then they're not First Runes."

"Nevertheless, I must pass."

"Only a Most-Beloved may pass."

Talon sighed. "I realize that," he said, finally accepting the course that the Fates had set before him. "That is why I must pass."

It took a few moments, then it struck the sentries simultaneously just what Talon was suggesting. Everyone knew that the Fates had chosen to spare his life rather than take it on the day of his execution. By his own admission, he had been allowed to see the Topside, only so that he might return. And now Lindsay's loving hands had handed him the only thing that could truly undo the Downside, destroying its spirit far more effectively than any Topside invasion ever could—if the things he had read were true. The only way to know for sure was to see the unknowable secrets of the Place of First Runes for himself.

Only a Most-Beloved may pass.

Which meant, if Talon passed, he must therefore be Most-Beloved. And these sentries could make it so by the simple turn of a gas key.

It wasn't something he had sought after. He wasn't like Railborn, who was always propelled by his family's dream of greatness. But then, perhaps that's why it had fallen on Talon. The sentries hesitated, then the one to his right broke stance, lowered his sword, and pulled the key from around his neck. He stuck it in a small hole in the wall and turned it—and although the second sentry didn't help, he didn't kill the first sentry, either. Soon the thick carpet of flowing blue flame was flickering out. The second sentry grabbed an unlit torch from the wall and touched it to the last bit of flame before it was gone, then handed it to Talon. Now the corridor was lit a pale orange from the burning torch.

"Remember us, Talon," one of them said. "Remember us in future days."

Talon told them that he would, if indeed there were future days. Then he stepped forward across the hot stone floor and toward the Chamber beyond.

■ ■ ■

If the Downside had a soul, it resided in the Place of First Runes. It was lower than the low-dwellings of the Advisors. It was even lower than the Bot, and since only a Most-Beloved was allowed to enter, no one had set foot within its walls for more than a decade. Talon did not know what he would find, and the fear of this ultimate unknown almost made him turn back—but his shoes had just about burned through as he crossed the thirty yards of hot floor that led to the Chamber, and he didn't know if he could stand the trip back until the floor cooled. It occurred to him that perhaps the flaming floor's purpose was not only to deter people from entering, but also to prevent those who did enter from turning back once they had made their choice.

He swallowed his fear and stepped forward into the Place of First Runes, not knowing what to expect, and not expecting what he saw.

It was a simple chamber, about a hundred feet long, and half as wide. The ceiling was low—just about a foot above his head. It was not paved in gold, or decorated in glistening jewels—and yet it was far from ordinary.

The place seemed neither Topside nor Downside in nature, but a combination of both. Everything was carved of marble and dusty granite. There were large rectangular stone boxes, and heavy monolithic markers—some squared off at the top, others fashioned into crosses. There were words carved into the stones, but there were also all manner of graffiti written everywhere as well—not the fine, intricate runes that Downsiders wrote, but sloppy scrawlings that told of events dated in Topside years, *old* Topside years, like the ones in the pages Lindsay had given him: 1895, 1901. A sinking feeling took hold in the pit of his stomach, and he decided not to fight it. He had come here to know the truth. He would not hide his eyes from it now, no matter how it made him feel.

It then occurred to Talon just what this place was. He had passed through one like it during his short stay on the Topside. He had almost slept there until he had realized with a morbid chill exactly what it was for.

This was a place for the dead.

The Champ had told him that the Topside remanded their dead to the ground rather than to the waters. He hadn't believed it until he had seen such a place for himself. But here, in the Downside, was a graveyard that must have dated back to the days before the Aquatorium. Talon counted thirty-nine graves, each bearing a Topside name.

He half-expected the spirits of the entombed to rise up in

a chorus of rage at having been disturbed. But if so, their rage would be well-matched by the rage growing within Talon.

At the far end of the Chamber was a monument larger and more elegant than the others. With his torch already beginning to fade, Talon made his way toward it. Columns rose on either side of a marble vault set into the wall. It was the only grave that had not been marred with the painted histories that filled almost every other surface of the room. There were, however, some words carved in the stone. Talon brushed the dust away and leaned close to read what he already knew it would say:

ALFRED ELY BEACH

❖

BORN: SEPTEMBER 1, 1826
DIED: AUGUST 5, 1902

❖

MOST BELOVED
OF ALL THOSE WHO DWELL
IN THE DOWNSIDE OF THE CITY.

So it was true. It was right there before him, carved in the stone of the Downside's most sacred place—a place that now no longer seemed sacred, but profane. He would have set the grave ablaze if there were something there to burn.

"We are a proud and noble people!" Talon screamed to the long-dead inventor. *"We have always been here! We will always be here."*

The words held no sway anymore. Because another voice

was speaking in his thoughts now, taunting, and tormenting. *We are nothing,* the voice told him. *We come from nothing. And we will always be...nothing.*

Talon left the Place of First Runes a few minutes later, his anger and anguish igniting an entirely new course of action. Still clutching the folder of truths in his hands, he set out to gather as many Downsiders as he could, to put a new plan into effect—a plan that would end, once and for all, this so-called "war" with the Topside.

No Topside army would set foot in their caverns. Their homes would not be pillaged, their chambers would not be turned into museums for Topside amusement. If all went according to plan, the Topside would be left with no further reason to dig...

...because if the Downside had to die, they would blow it up themselves.

18

The Left Half of Memory

The Aztecs no longer exist.

At face value, one might think this a good thing, because their practice of mass human sacrifice wasn't exactly a charming highlight of history…but on the other hand, every culture has nasty skeletons in its historical closet: sacrifices, slavery, Elvis impersonators—and who is to say if the Aztec gods might not have lost their thirst for blood had the conquistadores not flattened them under their armored feet.

But, unfortunately for Elvis and the Aztecs, the way we die is the way we are remembered—just as "the King" will be forever clad in the hideous rhinestones and white bell-bottoms of the seventies, the Aztecs' rich culture will always be overshadowed by the human hearts they served to Quetzalcoatl. Perhaps that is the greatest crime of conquest—that a civilization is denied the right to evolve beyond its own embarrassment.

It may be true that some milestones in history are inevitable; events that stand like great boulders in the flow of time that no amount of wisdom can avoid. But there are other times that the course of history turns in the hands of individuals....

■ ■ ■

The Downsiders were neither stupid nor suicidal, but they *were* desperate. So desperate that they clung to the convictions of a fourteen-year-old boy who had survived his own execution.

With word spreading that Talon had dared to enter the Chamber of First Runes, people twenty and thirty years his senior looked on him with a reverence that he ignored. Instead, he reined their awe into cooperation. Talon's plan was simple, his passion persuasive—and the Wise Advisors dared not oppose him, for Topsiders had already breached some of the outer tunnels, and time was short. Soon Talon had gathered all the tappers, and in turn they gathered every other Downsider who could be put to the task. Even little Pidge helped, sacrificing one of her prized playthings for the good of all.

As the gas tappers went out to begin their fearsome undertaking, the rest of the Downside gathered in the Floodgate Concourse, deep within the inner core of the Downside world. With mattresses torn from the Chamber of Soft Walls, entrances to the Concourse were tightly plugged to keep everyone within the Concourse safe from the cataclysm about to sweep through the High Perimeter. Word throughout the crowded cavern was that the Fates had spoken to Talon and told him that the only way to save the Downside was through a trial by fire. Talon didn't argue with them because perhaps they were right. Perhaps the Fates didn't speak in words but in turns of the heart. He wondered if he would have considered this course of action if he had not been exposed to the brutal truth of their own history—the folder that he still clutched in his hands as he waited for the High Perimeter to be flooded with methane.

When the last of the tappers returned, the final doorway was sealed. "We've closed all doors and hatches to the High Perimeter," one of the gas tappers reported, "but there's no telling how many of them will hold."

If they did hold, the high-perimeter tunnels would collapse, sealing out the Topside once and for all...but if those doors and hatches blew, there was no telling how much of the Downside would be lost as well.

"We'll be safe in here," the tappers assured everyone, but Talon wondered how certain they were.

As families huddled together, Talon found himself just a kid once more, clinging to his sister, and to his parents, who held them both in their frightened but protective arms and whispered words of comfort.

Meanwhile, in a High-Perimeter tunnel, where natural gas and oxygen had blended in lethal proportions, Pidge's old battery-operated puppy, the soles of its feet covered with gritty matchbook friction-strips, slowly shuffled its way toward a forest of matches.

■ ■ ■

Lindsay Matthias's eyes snapped open after hours of anesthetic sleep that passed in a dreamless instant. The electricity was still out, but the sun was now high in the sky. Usually morning light would always bring her clarity and a sense of peace, but today it brought a bleak and weighty cloud of regret. She had left Talon with her head held high, confident that her actions would bring about some glorious reconciliation of the two worlds. But what on earth had made her think such a reconciliation would be glorious—or that one was even needed? She had been so excited to uncover the truth of how the Downside came to be that she rode the fever of that excitement, only to realize that she had brought them a disease as virulent as smallpox. Yes, she had discovered the truth—but there were other truths as well—like the dignity the Downsiders had found; the passion and purity with which they lived their lives. What gave her the right to hold her truth above theirs?

Stormed by the Topside and stripped of their convictions, what would the Downsiders become under the heel of Topside life? She already knew the answer: They would be seen as insignificant curiosities, impoverished and pitifully ignorant. How long until the Downsiders saw themselves that way as well, becoming an underclass of destitute souls—the same way they had started more than a hundred years before?

With these thoughts brewing, she went downstairs to find Todd snoring on the couch, and her father sitting at the kitchen table, staring at nothing in particular.

This was the first sign that something was horribly wrong in her own little world as well, for usually her father was a body-in-motion, always running from one thing to another. But now he sat with a sense of inertia so heavy, he might as well have been shackled to the kitchen chair. The second sign that something was amiss were the chocolate bars—or at least the wrappers. It was no secret that her father was a chocoholic, but usually he could keep his cravings under control. Here on the table, however, was a wasteland of brown-and-silver Hershey's bar wrappers—just as there had been on that night so many years ago when he and her mother had decided to divorce. As on that day, the green-gilled dyspeptic look on her father's face had little to do with the bubbling cauldron of chocolate in his stomach. He now resided beneath his own black cloud as well, and Lindsay idly wondered if their two clouds could coexist in the same room without generating a thunderstorm.

She sat down across from him, although she had no idea what to say. She wasn't even sure she wanted to know what this particular Hershey Horror was about—such was the distance that had fallen between them in the weeks since her arrival.

"I thought you'd still be out with the rest of the city's engineers," she said. "Digging for gophers."

He shook his head. "They're not interested in my help," he told her. "They just want someone to blame."

"Blame?" That caught Lindsay by surprise. It never occurred to her that her father might end up taking the brunt of this utility disaster. True, her father *was* indirectly responsible for the city's woes by having dug the Westside Aqueduct Shaft in the first place—but no one on the surface could know that. "How can they blame you? That's ridiculous," she told him, as if dismissing it would make the problem go away.

"People don't care who gets blamed, just as long as somebody does." He picked up another chocolate bar, considered eating it, but gave it to Lindsay instead. "The fact is, *I* was the one uprooting the city's infrastructure, and *I* was the one who lost a truck down the shaft. My butt was a target the size of New Jersey, just waiting to get kicked."

"You really think they'll kick it?"

"They already have." Then he cleared away the wrappers before him to reveal a piece of official city stationery beneath it. The letter written on the paper bore a single line, and a space for her father's signature.

"They've requested my resignation."

Lindsay noticed a pen near the letter of resignation, lethally poised like a pistol. She wondered how long her father had been sitting there, contemplating that pen.

He blinked slowly, as if even his own eyelids were now a burden. "I put five years into building this aqueduct. Now they're taking it away from me..." His voice trailed off, and his gaze turned to the pen.

Perhaps it was the knowledge of what else was at stake today in the tunnels down below, or perhaps some of Todd's insensitivity had finally rubbed off on her, but Lindsay found herself wanting to shake her father. *It's just a hole in the ground,* she wanted to say...but as she looked at him, she realized it wasn't just the hole he was seeing. He was seeing everything else that would be sucked into that hole: his career, his home, but most of all, his dignity. And it occurred to Lindsay that he wasn't all that different from Talon—for her father, too, would be losing his world today.

For the first time in as long as she could remember, Lindsay wanted to reach across that precarious chocolate wrapper chasm to him, but she had no idea what she could do or say. She couldn't share with him her own woes and misgivings...she couldn't tell him about the Downside...but as she thought about it, she realized she did have something they could share that could bridge the distance between them.

There was the box in her suitcase.

She had hidden it so well, she had almost forgotten about it. Without a word, she left her father and went up to her room. Then, standing on her desk chair, she pulled the suitcase off a closet shelf and fished out the shoe box, which was creased and dented from the trip out from Texas and her own weeks of neglect. She didn't have to look inside—she had done that enough before she arrived, and she knew every item inside. Looking at them had been like scratching a scab—knowing it would bleed, yet unable to stop. She was supposed to have presented these items to her father upon her arrival. Instead, she had taken guilty pleasure in hiding them...for in its own way, the box was a letter of resignation, too—one that she had no desire to deliver.

When she returned to the kitchen, her father was still there, contemplating the pen. She sat down and set the shoe box between them. "Mom said you should have this," she told him, then opened the box to reveal her mother's parting gift to both of them.

Inside were a dozen incomplete items. The left half of memories.

There was a single champagne glass—half of a set her parents had sipped from on the day they were wed. There was Lindsay's baby book—an oddly slim thing that on closer inspection revealed itself to be only half the book, neatly rebound to hide the fact that every other page was missing. There was one pink baby bootie—part of a pair Lindsay had worn shortly after the exaggerated forty-eight hours of labor her mother claimed to have endured. There were other things, too—from keys for locks that no longer existed, to a ceramic bookend with no mate.

She wanted to hate her mother for dividing these memories, but then she considered the care with which they had been prepared and packed. Her mother had done this painstakingly, with great attention to the gravity of her task. She had cleanly separated the inseparable, like a surgeon transplanting a heart.

Now the other half of this collection was part of another world, and although Lindsay never expected her parents' two worlds to be reconciled, neither did she want to admit that they would be eternally separate. Lindsay tried to imagine her mother somewhere in the Serengeti looking at her half of this final settlement of accounts. Did her mother even take them with her, or were they like the furniture she left behind in the dark limbo of storage? Well, maybe some truths *were* better left unknown.

Her father looked at the box, but did not attempt to remove anything, as if it were some sort of diorama—a fragile shadowbox to be seen, but not touched....

So Lindsay reached in and pulled out the pink knit booty. "I'm sorry for the things that have been taken from you, Daddy," she said, then she reached out and pressed the tiny knit sock into his hand. "Maybe this can make up for it."

For the longest time he rubbed it between his thumb and forefinger, staring at it, saying nothing. Then he looked at the pen. Perhaps it was just her imagination, but it seemed to Lindsay that the pen no longer held the same malevolence it had only a moment ago. He picked it up and, in one smooth, confident motion, signed his name to the letter of resignation, as if that particular loss was now unimportant. And he smiled.

Far away there was a distant rumble, like the foundation shifting. The walls rattled for an instant, and a report came up from the drain, like a hollow belch from the center of the earth. But even then, Lindsay and her father continued to share their moment of silence, if for no other reason than to honor the memory of all the worlds lost to the passing of time.

Fire in the Hole

In its pure state, natural gas has no odor—its unpleasant stench has to be added, to make gas leaks easy to smell. Few Topsiders had their olfactory sense more attuned to changes in atmosphere than those whose jobs took them beneath the city streets, for down below, a keen sense of smell could mean the difference between life and death.

Shortly before Lindsay's walls rattled and her drains belched, a dozen tireless teams of city workers had begun to break through the Downside barricades, into tunnels that seemed remarkably well maintained—tunnels that seemed to lead inward toward some other place entirely. Just as their curiosity began to take hold, drawing their thoughts deeper into the mysteries that lay ahead, their noses caught the unmistakable smell of leaking gas. When they were faced with a maddened scurry of rats racing past to seek better air, they didn't wait to find the source of the gas leak. Each and every team turned tail, abandoning their curiosity along with their equipment, and joined the rat race in a mad dash for the surface.

As they ran, they heard the gas ignite somewhere deep down, and they could hear the series of explosions drawing nearer, moving just behind the speed of sound. By the time they emerged into daylight, they knew there was no time to do anything but dive for cover.

Few people, however, had a better view of the catastrophe than Becky Peckerling—whose eyewitness account would make her the most popular girl at Icharus Academy for some time to come.

Becky was making her way from her West Side apartment to her Saturday violin lesson, fuming over the fact that this utility crisis didn't come close enough to hell freezing over for her instructor to cancel the lesson. Around her, traffic police had replaced the unlit streetlights. Word was that traffic was at a standstill around the city's bridges and tunnels, where impatient citizens were making hasty escapes. But here, on the West Side, traffic was actually less busy than on a typical Saturday.

The policeman had just blown his whistle and signaled for her to cross the street, when the ground began to shake with the force of an earthquake. All at once a blast of light and heat hit her from the right, and she turned to see, several blocks away, a cloud of fire erupt from a construction site, sending dump trucks and all sorts of other heavy equipment flying through the air like Tonka toys.

That's the Aqueduct Shaft! she thought to herself just as the sound from the blast hit her like a sonic boom, rattling her braces and purging all thoughts from her mind. She stood there in the middle of the street, watching the fireball rise and facing an approaching procession of exploding manhole covers, which popped from the ground like corks from champagne as the underground shock wave moved closer. Then, when she looked down, she noticed that her own feet were standing squarely on a manhole cover.

One block away another manhole blew, and then another half a block away. Needless to say, Becky was not in an enviable position—and although her instinct for survival was less developed than some, she did manage to sidestep off the manhole cover just before it blew sky-high with a fiery burst that melted the nylon off the right sleeve of her jacket. As she fell to the ground, she caught sight of that manhole cover flipping through the air like a two-hundred-pound coin, and she knew it had to come down somewhere. She got up screaming, convinced that no matter where she ran, that manhole cover would land squarely on her head, as punishment for all her years of prattling chatter. When the manhole landed a healthy twenty feet away, she was relieved, but also a bit disappointed that the Powers-That-Be did not find her worthy of smiting in a freak accident.

Then, in the silence just after the explosion, it began to rain—but it wasn't the kind of rain that any weatherman would predict. It pummeled the streets around Becky with a jangling clatter, and shone in the air as it fell, like shimmering bits of sun. It was more like hail. It struck her head and arms, stinging like snaps from a rubber band, so she held her violin case above her head to protect herself from the falling sky.

Around her the street began to glimmer bronze, and she dared to reach out to catch one of these hailstones in her hand only to discover that it wasn't hail at all. "Hmm," said Becky, "that's odd."

It appeared that today's prevailing weather condition called for only the sturdiest of umbrellas—because today, it was raining subway tokens.

On the Dark Side
of the Moon

Just a few short hours after the Aqueduct Shaft blew, the utilities were all restored as unexpectedly as they had gone out, and the current of traffic flowing out of the city reversed direction, heading right back in. The time was, according to every digital appliance in the city, 12:00, in urgent blinking green.

In a world addicted to change and new experiences, current events become yesterday's news before nightfall. Only a scant few events become legendary. The legend of the Great Shaft Disaster, was, like most legends, made up of a few bare facts, upon which were hung the most outlandish speculation. The most common version of the legend is this: Evil city engineer Mark Matthias, while digging the Aqueduct Shaft, came across some key pressure points for the city's entire utility structure. At that point, he may or may not have blackmailed city hall, threatening to shut the city down. A dump truck, which may or may not have been filled with the city's ransom payment, had the bad fortune to fall into the hole, revealing that the alleged bags of ransom loot were actually just bags of worthless old subway tokens. Then, after spreading some cockamamy story about an underground cavern, with archaeological "experts" who may or may not have been his partners in crime, Matthias made good his threat to shut down the city. In the end it took a highly covert military operation to collapse the shaft, and sever Matthias's stranglehold on the city.

Of course none of this could be substantiated—all people knew for sure was that Matthias resigned amidst a storm of controversy—but everyone had heard the blackmail story from their hairdresser, or their dentist, or their hairdresser's dentist—and the fact that city hall flatly denied it made people believe it even more.

The one Topside girl who knew the truth knew she could share it with no one. Although Lindsay longed to know the fate of the Downside, and although she wanted to spare her father from the absurdly spiraling rumors about his involvement, she also knew that she was the keeper of their secret. Not a day passed where she didn't worry about the fate of Talon and the Downside—that they indeed might have drowned in Lindsay's waves, as the Champ had warned. It was only her trust in Talon and his ability to rise above—or more accurately, sink below—that gave her hope.

At first she found herself horrified by the whispered allegations against her father, but soon her father found himself amused by it. After all, his only ambition had been to supply the city with water for the next five hundred years, and now he was being treated like a villain of James Bond-like pro-portions—a status, incidentally, that commanded far more respect than he had ever had before.

"I enjoy being infamous," he told Lindsay over dinner one night. "The bank tellers know my name."

As it turned out, that same infamy was enough to extract Todd's mother from her comfortable Brooklyn cult. Refusing to allow her son to remain in the clutches of an evil stepfather, she came to collect him, then promptly shipped him off to a brutal military academy upstate, where all the food was in lumpy shades of brown, and "personal space" meant the three feet of air between an upper and a lower bunk. Whenever Lindsay got to feeling blue, she thought of Todd doing push-ups at five A.M., and scrubbing bathroom floors with his toothbrush. It always made her feel better.

Yet each day she would find herself peering into air vents, storm drains, sewer grates, and every dark, unknown place she came across for a sign that the Downsiders were still there, refusing to believe the explosion had destroyed them. She returned to the library time and again, only to be ejected from the lower vaults by security before she could get anywhere close to the Downside. She had gone down to the shaft site, but what little remained of the shaft had been filled in, paved as a parking lot, and forgotten. The subway tokens that hadn't been taken as souvenirs were carried off by pigeons, leaving nothing but the scratches and dings in metal awnings to testify that brass had ever rained at all.

It wasn't until April that Lindsay came across a curious report in the news—something described as an April Fools' Day joke. Apparently librarians had been finding numerous volumes missing from every section of the library's main branch. With a library of so many millions of volumes, the disappearances could have gone unnoticed for months…if it hadn't been for the fact that each missing book was replaced by a single sock. And no two of the socks matched.

■ ■ ■

What did it take to end the World? The Topside knew—in fact, it was skilled in inventing scenarios. As every six-year-old could tell you, everything from nuclear apocalypse to a microbiologic epidemic could bring about an effective Topside end. The Downside, however, being so much smaller, did not need such elaborate methods. Their end could be far more modest.

On that dark day, after the explosions had subsided and the mattresses were pulled from the Floodgate Concourse doors, Talon expected everything to be gone. He was half right.

The Hot Springs and the Hudward Growing Caverns had caved in. So had the batward dwellings, the Lesser Rune Chambers, and everything within a thousand paces of the Brass Junction. A full half of the Downside was gone. But that meant that half was spared—and even though the entire batward end of the Bot had collapsed, the herd was yonkward that day.

Against their own better judgment, but deferring to Talon's wishes, the tappers immediately restored the Topside's utilities, rerouting it around the blast zone to make certain every last Topsider could bathe, flush, broil, and dial once more. And to everyone's amazement, the Topsiders abandoned the war, becoming as complacent and lethargic as they had been before, so bloated on electricity, gas, water, and the sounds of their own voices that they didn't bother to wage further war. They left the Downside alone to deal with their biggest remaining problem: the population crunch caused by half the living space.

Now, as things slowly began to return to normal, Talon discovered what a Most-Beloved was required to do. Which was nothing in particular. Since nothing in particular was an easy task to excel in, his adjustment was remarkably easy.

They had wanted to build him his own new low-dwelling, but what with people setting up housekeeping in passageways, he had no business accepting such an offer. He refused, telling them that at the very most he needed nothing more than a thicker curtain between his and his parents' rooms.

It was on the day that the curtain was to be delivered—in a quiet moment, almost two months after the "war"—that Talon allowed himself to think of Lindsay. In truth, he thought of her often, but he always found good reason to chase the thought away. After all, rebuilding a world took far more effort than blowing it up. But today he let her memory play in his thoughts as he held in his hands the time bomb she had given him: a folder that he had carefully sewn into his pillow. He had yet to share Lindsay's truth with anyone. There was an anger he felt toward her, that she would give him such earth-shattering information, and yet an even deeper gratitude that she cared enough to make such a hard choice. Of course, she wasn't being entirely selfless, but she wasn't being entirely selfish, either. It was very human of her, and he held on to the folder, because he couldn't hold on to her.

His mother pushed back the curtain and stepped in. Almost reflexively Talon began to squeeze the pillow tighter in his hands, as if it were a rabid rat that could leap out of his arms and attack her.

"Skeet's here with the new curtain," his mother told him. "He wants the honor of hanging it himself."

Talon grimaced as the memory of Railborn and Gutta struck him like the pang of a healing wound. Skeet Skinner, bearing the weight of his son's disappearance, had taken it upon himself to gather the finest patches from the finest skins and oversee the creation of a leather curtain for the new Most-Beloved. It was far more than Talon wanted, but he could not refuse the gift.

Talon concealed his grimace with an apologetic grin. "Tell Skeet he can hang the curtain in a few minutes." The admiration of the entire Downside was a poor substitute for lost friends. He had to believe that Railborn hadn't just "wandered the wrong way" with Gutta, as Strut Mason claimed. He had to believe that Railborn chose to save her life, and that they were together in a sort of permanent Topside rotation—a challenge he knew they would both rise to.

Talon's mother turned to leave, but thought better of it, then turned to him and said, "Those papers in your pillow—are they Topside?"

The question knocked the wind out of Talon. At first he

tried to hide his reaction, and then realized there was no point, for when had he ever successfully concealed anything from her?

"Yes and no," he answered truthfully.

"I was tempted to read them, but then decided if they were important enough to guard even in your sleep, perhaps I'd better leave them be."

He looked down at the pillow, so ineffectively concealing its load. "I don't know what to do with them."

"You'll figure it out," she told him with absolute certainty.

The fact was, he already had figured it out...but knowing what he had to do and actually doing it were two different things.

His mother shook her head and laughed. "My son the Most-Beloved. If I had thought it six months ago, I would have been bounding the soft walls." Then her laughter faded, and she gazed at him as if she were searching for something she could not find. "Nowadays, Talon...when I look at you, it's as if you're a stranger to me. Like I don't even know you anymore."

Six months ago, he would have been happy to hear her say that...but now he told her, in the quietest of voices, "Please, Mom. I need you to know me just a little while longer."

And although nothing else was said, Talon knew she understood.

■　■　■

Alfred Ely Beach's grave was just as Talon had left it. The only difference was that now there was no need to convince the guards to douse the flames and let him pass—although they did look at each other curiously when they noticed the pillow he carried under his arm.

As he knelt beside the grave, he laid the torch on the ground. It was already fading, but he would take his time in doing this. Respect was owed to the First Most-Beloved of the Downside, even if the respect could come from no one but Talon.

"You would be proud of us," Talon said, speaking to the long-dead inventor. "We have honor, we have compassion… but most of all, we have self-respect. I guess we didn't have that on the Topside. I guess that is why we chose to stay down here."

At the edge of the grave was something Talon hadn't noticed on his first visit. It was a journal so covered in dust, it just about blended into the ground around it. The book must have detailed those first years, and how Beach's great train project had evolved into the creation of this world instead. Although Talon was tempted, he did not open the journal, nor did he read the many writings on the walls. It was enough to know they were there.

"You would have been proud of us," he said again. "And I hope you'll understand what I have to do now." Then Talon tore apart his pillow, scattering feathers across the grave. He pulled out the folder Lindsay had given him, all wrinkled and stained from many weeks of late-night sweats. He straightened the pages as best he could, and laid them down beside the journal.

"You had to be forgotten, or the Downside wouldn't take. You knew that, didn't you?" Talon tried to imagine that first generation a hundred years ago, suffering to erase its own true history and lovingly building a false history for the sake of their children, and their children's children. A world based on a lie...and yet the Downside turned that lie into something glorious. If they could save a faller with the touch of a sword, surely that lie deserved to be knighted into truth.

"I will be keeper of your secret," Talon told the silent grave of the forgotten inventor. "I will be the one who remembers why we forget."

The torch went out, but Talon lingered in the darkness. Truth was such a strange thing—its face changing depending on the angle at which it was viewed. There were some truths that gained value by being proclaimed, and others whose greatest virtue is that they remain unknown. Better that the truth be like the moon, which Talon had so briefly spied above the Topside night—a bright sphere only showing half of its face at a time, leaving the rest to be uncovered fragment by fragment, in its own proper time.

"Someday there will come a time for us to know...," said Talon. "But there are many more things we must know first." If there was one thing he had learned from his trip to the surface, it was the vastness of their own ignorance. There were those who couldn't see this; those who said, "Forget the Topside, and dig deeper still. Teach our children that the Topside doesn't even exist." But burrowing into deeper darkness was no more a solution than was exposing themselves to the blinding truth of how their world came to be. Perhaps, thought Talon, there was a path in between. A way to shed their ignorance without losing their souls.

Talon touched the grave that now stretched invisibly before him, leaving his handprint firmly in the dust as a sign that he had been there, then he left.

Once across the steaming pumice approach, he instructed the sentries, in the sternest voice that a fourteen-year-old could muster, that the fire be turned back on, and that no one—not even he—be allowed to enter the Place of First Runes again until many years hence, when the next Most-Beloved demanded their glimpse of the unknowable.

■ ■ ■

Meanwhile, about as far from the Downside as the moon itself, sat Long Island, completely unknown to them, and the type of place Downside map makers would label HERE BE DRAGONS.

On Long Island's North Shore, about thirty miles away from anything Downside, was the John Alden Dix Home for wards of the state—a pleasant enough place, as far as orphanages go, with a nice view of Long Island Sound, and the distant Throgsneck Bridge, the name of which was lost on most of Dix Home's residents.

The teenagers wing was filled with kids bitter about the fact that they were never adopted—but many were now drawing strength from two newcomers, a boy and a girl who shared a closeness that was the envy of their peers. Although they chose to keep their past a mystery, Raymond, as he called himself, proved to be a wizard at navigating the blind passageways of the Internet, hunting down information as if he were born to it. The girl, Greta, although still recovering from unexplained wounds, managed to defuse every conflict that arose among the angrier kids in the home with an empathetic and rational ear that could someday make her a master diplomat.

There was no question that the two were the most beloved kids in the home.

The Highside

With April came windswept days when the storm clouds shred into skies full of bright, billowing islands. Days when schoolchildren ran across the Great Lawn of Central Park, holding their jackets open like bat wings, daring the spring wind to give them flight. It was on a day like this, when anything seemed possible, that Lindsay saw Talon once again.

"I hate windy days," Becky Peckerling complained as she and Lindsay walked home from school. Becky held down her skirt, which the wind kept trying to lift. Lindsay smiled at her frustrated attempts to keep the wind from its mischief.

"Actually, I like the wind," she told Becky. "I like what it does to my hair."

"It makes you look like Einstein."

This time Lindsay did laugh. Months ago, in those days when her hair was a taut gator-tail braid, the thought of her hair unkempt and windblown would have mortified her, but not now. So many things had changed since her arrival in December—but in a way it was oddly comforting to know that Becky hadn't.

Of course, Becky did have her fifteen minutes of Icharus Academy fame after her eyewitness account of the Torrent of Tokens. She would pick through her braid-parted scalp as if hunting for lice, to show awestruck schoolmates the actual red marks where the tokens had struck her. She still had those red marks, although Lindsay suspected she was now making those marks herself, and would probably continue to do so until people stopped asking to see them.

As they crossed Third Avenue, Lindsay heard someone call her name. It wasn't the first time, either—she had thought she'd heard it a few streets back, but it was so faint, she had been certain it was her imagination. This time, she wasn't so sure. She spun on her heel, but saw no one there.

"Did you hear that?" she asked Becky, who said she could hear nothing over the honking horns. At first Lindsay thought it might have come from a passing car, but then she noticed, a few yards away, an open manhole marked off with orange traffic cones and a big MEN AT WORK sign. A hint of excitement relayed up her spine and back down again until she could feel it tingling in her toes. There was no one near the manhole, and further down the street she spied a group of city workers near a van, drinking coffee and joking, making it very clear that the Men at Work, in fact, weren't.

Lindsay strode to the manhole and peered in, while Becky, who was no friend to manholes, kept her distance.

"Did you drop something, Lindsay? I didn't see you drop

anything. Maybe you left it at school. Maybe it's in your locker."

"I didn't drop anything, Becky."

To Becky's growing horror, Lindsay leaned further over the hole. All she could see was a brick-lined shaft and a rusted ladder descending into darkness. She thought she heard her name again, but the roar of a passing truck made it hard to be sure.

"The light is about to change," Becky warned. She glanced warily at a cab still stopped at the light, gunning its engine, preparing to charge. "Lindsay—I don't like the look of that cabbie. He looks psychotic."

Lindsay got down on her knees and pulled her hair away from her eyes as she peered into the hole. Then at last she caught sight of two points of light deep down in the shadows. A pair of eyes reflecting the light of day.

The light changed, the cabbie swerved around them within an inch of their lives, and Becky took refuge behind the MEN AT WORK sign.

"Lindsay, are you trying to kill us?" she asked.

To which Lindsay replied, "Becky, I have to go now." And she climbed down into the hole, vanishing beneath Third Avenue.

Becky lingered through two traffic light cycles and several more psychotic cabbies. But in the end she finally gave up, determined that the next time she walked home with Lindsay, *she* would be the one to unexpectedly crawl into some ungodly hole, and let's just see how Lindsay liked it, hmm?

■ ■ ■

NEAL SHUSTERMAN

Twenty rungs down, the manhole ended at a circular drainage tunnel, and standing there, as she knew he would be, was Talon.

"It's about time you heard me," he said. "I've been calling you for three grates and two storm drains." Although his words were reserved, he couldn't hide his excitement at seeing her. Even in this dim light, she could see it in his eyes.

"It's Topside custom to say hello when you greet someone," said Lindsay. "Especially someone who thought you were dead."

"I'm not dead," he told her in all seriousness, "just very busy."

She laughed, threw her arms around him, and was pleased to feel him return the embrace.

"Do you have any idea how hard you were to find?" he asked.

"We had to move to a smaller place," said Lindsay. "It's lucky you found me at all." But it was less lucky than she would have had him believe...because she often went out of her way to travel the same path she used to take home, on the off chance that someone who knew that path might just be observing her from a rain gutter.

"You're not the only one who's moved," said Talon. "I haven't been able to find The Champ anywhere."

"Neither have I," said Lindsay. Of course, she *had* heard rumors of someone setting up house in an old, dry-docked submarine in some abandoned shipyard...."Perhaps we could look for him together."

Talon thought about it for a moment, then took her hand. "Come on, there's something I want to show you." He led her, as he had once before, through the darkest of tunnels weaving deep beneath the city. But this time those tunnels felt different. First was the smell. Everything smelled of smoke and ash, like a fireplace the day after Christmas. The walls weren't right, either—they were rough and jagged to the touch, as if they were not so much walls but piles of debris. Talon moved more slowly than he had on her previous visit, as if these places were not the same ones he was used to.

"Where are you taking me?"

"You'll see."

In spite of the destruction she sensed all around her, Talon's voice was cheery and light. "I'm sorry your father won't get his underground river," he said.

"That's okay—he was just hired to design a water-park—you know, with wave pools and water-slides." She could feel his sudden shiver move through her, but decided not to ask what that was about. "Anyway, he's building it in the parking lot of the aqueduct horse-racing track—so I guess he'll get his aqueduct after all."

"You people race horses?" Talon asked, and when she told him yes, he asked her what a horse was.

"Next time you and your friends raid the library," she said, "you might want to check out a book on animals."

He stopped short. "How did you find out about that?"

"I used my Topside wiles."

He led her up a damaged ladder, and then another, until they came into a space where the smell of ash was not as strong. Then, to her surprise, he flicked a switch, and a fluorescent bulb flickered awake above them to reveal they were in some sort of basement.

NEAL SHUSTERMAN

"This is it?" she asked. "There's nothing here!"

"We're not there yet."

Now that she could see him in the light, there was something about him that seemed a bit different, although she couldn't quite say what it was.

They went up some metal stairs—but not just one flight. The gray steel steps switchbacked up and up, from one landing to another, until Lindsay felt her ears begin to pop. "Are we still in the Downside?"

"Of course we are."

They climbed so high, Lindsay's legs grew weary—almost fifteen minutes, until the stairs came to an end at a door that said NO ADMITTANCE. From his waist Talon pulled out what looked like a baseball cap but was of definite Downside design—a quilt sewn of a hundred tiny pieces of shredded fabric, all lighter shades than the earth tones of the rest of his clothes. Talon slipped on the cap, then pushed the door open and the wind took over, swinging the door wide.

And once again, Lindsay stepped over the threshold into another world.

Before them was a huge platform, and around it heavy columns held up a domed roof that must have been five stories high. On the platform sat two immense water tanks—black iron things at least thirty feet around and forty feet high. They looked like two giant coffee cans sitting on a stage. Although the tanks were partially enclosed by the pillars and roof, they were also open to the outside. It was like a bell tower with pillars and a roof, but no walls, and when Lindsay looked out, she could see the city stretching out before her. They were downtown, atop one of the city's older skyscrapers, the kind faced with stone and brick instead of chrome and glass.

"It fits all the rules for Downside territory," said Talon. "No Topsider has come up here for years—and they never actually go *into* the cisterns." He looked at the two towering water tanks. "The water level in these cisterns never goes higher than halfway—so we built a second floor above the water." He pointed to the first tank, then the second. "My parents will live in this one, and my sister and I will have that one—and we have all this space around us for our sitting room. As for those fire stairs we came up, Topsiders won't go near them unless the building burns down—so we can use them to go back under for market day, or meetings, or any other time we'd rather be down."

Although Lindsay was as quick-witted as they come, on this matter she was slow on the uptake, convinced that she must not have heard Talon correctly. "You mean Downsiders...up here?"

"Of course it wasn't easy to convince everyone—but after two months of living cramped in together, they were ready to consider it."

"But...but what about the sun? Downsiders aren't allowed to see the sun!"

Talon grinned more broadly than Lindsay had ever seen him smile before. "Things change."

And then Lindsay realized what was different about Talon. He had a tan.

"I convinced them that the sky isn't really a part of the Topside—it's above it—and we have every right to it, too,

NEAL SHUSTERMAN

just like the water or the electricity. And so now we will live both below you...and above you!"

"It'll never work!"

"It already has."

He went to a mirror that was jury-rigged on a tripod by the edge of the roof. By angling it outward, he caught the sun and reflected it to the towers around them in a pattern that was something like Morse code.

And in a few moments, a tower three streets away flashed back the same greeting, and then another six blocks away.

Lindsay could only shake her head and let her jaw flap in the wind—something she knew was particularly unattractive, but her jaw had lost all communication with her brain.

"Fifty families on fifty roofs," he told her proudly. "And more to come. In fact, I wouldn't be surprised if all of us lived up here eventually."

"But...but aren't you worried that someone will catch you?" Yet even as Lindsay thought about it, she knew that no one would. How long had the Downside survived undetected just below the surface? Downsiders were practically invisible—and the truth was, their invisibility was powered by the Topside's desire not to see them. Who, really, would ever go searching in cisterns and the forgotten rooftops of aging towers? If they kept themselves out of the sight lines of neighboring tower windows, they could stay there...forever.

Lindsay felt a lump building in her throat. "So you will never let yourselves be known...."

Then Talon became a bit more solemn. "We will," he said.

"We will when we know all the things that you know. Only then can we face the Topside and not be swallowed by it."

"That could be years!" insisted Lindsay. "Lifetimes!"

But Talon pointed down at the Rolex still stretched around his ankle. "Time is of low importance."

"We could teach you—"

"No," he said flatly. "We will take our own knowledge. Otherwise, it means nothing."

Lindsay then dropped all pretenses, and asked the question that they both knew hid behind all the others.

"When will I see you again?"

Talon sighed, and gazed across the roof. "So many of these buildings look alike...but I'm sure you could find this building again if you needed to...."

Lindsay looked away as well. She knew what he was really saying. Yes, she could try to find this building from the surface, figuring out how it fit into the jagged puzzle of the city's skyline...but he was asking her *not* to find it. Because if his people were to survive, either in the depths below or in the rafters above, they had to be left alone. The touch of their worlds had almost destroyed them. The next time they touched, it would be on Downside terms.

It saddened Lindsay deeply to know that he would be so close, but always out of her grasp...and yet there was great joy in knowing that she had the strength to let him go.

Talon reached up and brushed a tear from her eye. She told him that it was just the wind, but of course he knew better. "My grandmother used to say that twisting paths always cross again," he told her. "And whose paths are more twisted than ours?"

Talon turned to the windswept sky, and it was then she noticed that the cap Talon wore wasn't sewn from fabric at all. It was made entirely of feathers. To imagine a feathered baseball cap, she would think it to be laughable—but not this cap. As with all other things, the Downside had created a thing of great value and beauty. White gull, gray pigeon, bluejay—every feather sewn so tightly to the next that it appeared to be a single fabric filled with many shades. It seemed so natural, so normal on him that there was no question where he belonged. He belonged up here.

Up above, the winds sliced through the clouds, tearing them into a mosaic of light. The setting sun turned the whole sky crimson, and the clouds shone an electric blue, bruising to violet. It was the kind of sunset that could stop traffic...but the drivers below were not looking up. Instead, they were leaning on their horns, making it clear to both Talon and Lindsay that no one would be found on the rooftops, for in the Topside, where time was of high importance, no one had the time to look.

Faced with the spectacle of the sunset, Talon's thoughts began to take flight. He had come here to impress Lindsay with what they had accomplished over these past few months. He never expected that *he* would be the one impressed, but as he stood there, he was transfixed by the glorious sky. He had seen the sky do many things since knowing it. He had seen it send rain, and flash with fire, then cough and grumble in angry complaint. He had seen it vanish, leaving nothing but a white ghost stretched from one end of the world to the other. And yes, he had seen at least a dozen sunsets, and no two were alike—but none had been like this. If there had ever been any doubt in his mind as to whether or not annexing the rooftops to the Downside was a good idea, those thoughts were now washed away. A sunset like this could only mean that, at last, the Fates were pleased, and the sky itself was welcoming them.

"I suppose you can't really call yourselves Downsiders anymore," said Lindsay.

Talon turned to her—it was something he had never considered. "So what might we be?"

"I'm not sure...I suppose you're 'Highsiders' now."

Talon smiled. "Highsiders," he said, testing the sound of the word, and the feel as it flowed from his tongue. "Highsiders...I like it!"

Dizzy from the shifting winds and the intoxicating colors, he sat down. Lindsay sat beside him, and he held her, for in such a moment, one simply *had* to hold, or be held—and although they didn't share the thought with one another, both were thinking the same thing: that if time began and ended in this moment, and if all of creation was just this instant in time, that would be fine. They could live with that.

Then, just before the colors of the sky began to fade, a thought occurred to Talon. "Lindsay," he said, "you don't suppose there might be *Skysiders*, too—people who walk on the dome of the sky?"

Lindsay smiled. "I don't know," she said. "Maybe..."

For who were they to doubt the possibilities?

NEAL SHUSTERMAN